THE DOMINO EFFECT

Ann Coburn

RED FOX

For my mother, Jean, with love.

A Red Fox Book

Published by Random House Children's Books
20 Vauxhall Bridge Road, London SW1V 2SA

A division of Random House UK Ltd
London Melbourne Sydney Auckland
Johannesburg and agencies throughout the world

Copyright © Ann Coburn 1994

1 3 5 7 9 10 8 6 4 2

First published by The Bodley Head Children's Books 1994

Red Fox edition 1996

Printed and bound in Great Britain by
Cox & Wyman Ltd, Reading, Berkshire

RANDOM HOUSE UK Limited Reg. No. 954009

Papers used by Random House UK Limited
are natural, recyclable products made from wood grown in
sustainable forests. The manufacturing processes conform to
the environmental regulations of the country of origin

ISBN 0 09 933691 X

THE DOMINO EFFECT

'Mum! What are you doing?'

Eleanor whirled around with the nail brush still clutched in one hand. Her lips and the skin around them were red and swollen from the scrubbing, but the rest of her face was deathly pale. Her black hair was plastered to her head and a thin line of blood trickled from a split in her lower lip.

Red as blood, white as snow, black as a crow's wing, thought Rowan, stupidly. Snow White. She shook the words away but they came back, beating in her head and making it hard to think.

'Mum?' she said, and her voice came out high and shaky, like a little girl's.

Eleanor licked the blood from her lower lip and turned her back. 'You go to bed. Let me have my bath. I'll – see you in the morning,' she said, in a voice that strained to be normal.

'But, Mum—'

'Go – let me—'

'Please, Mum—'

Eleanor's voice splintered. 'Go to bed! Get out and leave me alone!'

Also by Ann Coburn in Red Fox

Welcome to the Real World
The Granite Beast

The snow came slanting out of a heavy, grey sky that was clamped over the rim of the valley like a dustbin lid. As Rowan struggled up the hill, icy pellets blasted out of the gloom and raked across her face, making it difficult to see the road ahead. She remembered the man who had died in a blizzard up on the moors a few years back. He had left his car stuck in a drift and tried to walk back to the village he had just driven through. He was probably quite confident when he climbed out of his warm car and set off in his shiny black shoes and his smart suit and his sheepskin jacket. They had found him the next morning, far from the road, curled up in a bed of snow with his head pillowed on his briefcase.

What would it feel like, to freeze? Such a cold, blue death! Rowan pushed the thought away and concentrated on climbing the slippery path. At last she rounded the final bend in the road and walked towards the dark outline of the barn. Six months ago, she would have been glad to see the barn. Six months ago she had been as confident about her life as that man driving across the moor just before he buried the nose of his car in a snowdrift. She had been warm, happy, sure of the way ahead. Now, she was far from the road and very, very frightened. Rowan slowed, suddenly reluctant to reach the barn, but she made herself go on. She knew exactly what she had to do.

When she unlocked the back door, the kitchen was in darkness.

'Mum?' called Rowan.

A muffled reply came from the main room. Rowan stamped the snow from her boots and hurried across the kitchen. The main room was dark too. She jabbed at the light switch and turned to face her mother.

'Oh,' said Rowan softly. 'Oh, no.'

The place had been destroyed.

Their furniture was tumbled in a rough pile at the back of the room and the polished wooden floor where it had stood was covered in splintered glass and a thick layer of white dust. Rowan raised her gaze from the floor to the front of the room, where the great wall of windows looked out over the valley. One half of the glass was still shrouded in the make-shift curtain of old blankets and sheets that Eleanor had stapled together. Eleanor was standing there now, peering around the edge of the curtain at the snowy night. On the other half, the glass of every window had been smashed and the holes were covered with squares of plywood, nailed to the empty frames.

Rowan began to shake her head in horrified disbelief but stopped when she caught sight of the new brick wall under the lower edge of the plywood. It started at the original barn wall, where the raw red of the brick grated against the honey-coloured stone, and ran the whole width of the smashed windows.

Rowan walked over to the wall, her boots crunching through the splintered glass. She crouched and studied the bricks behind the plywood. Already the new wall was waist high. Rowan straightened, her nose filled with the cold, grey smell of wet mortar.

'Mum! What have you done?'

Eleanor turned from the window to face Rowan. She looked . . . what was the word? Damaged, that was it. She looked damaged. There was nothing obvious about it. Her bruises had faded months ago and, although the severely scraped back hair seemed to emphasize her paleness and the shadows under her eyes, on the outside she looked fine. This damage went deeper than bruises. It showed in the way she stood with her shoulders hunched and her arms folded across her heart. It showed in the way her glance darted everywhere, never quite meeting Rowan's gaze.

2

'What have you done?' repeated Rowan, forcing the harshness out of her voice.

'Don't you remember?' Eleanor said. 'I told you I was getting someone in to make this more permanent.' She reached out a hand to flick the blanket curtain.

'But – but I didn't think you meant walling us in! I thought you meant blinds, or something!'

'Oh, no. No, blinds wouldn't stop them,' said Eleanor, jerking her head at the darkness outside the windows. 'And I'm not walling us in. I've told the builders to leave the terrace doors. It wasn't very practical, was it, that great big wall of glass? We'll be much warmer with a proper wall there.' She gave a tight, little smile and turned back to her post. 'At least it's quiet out there tonight. No spies. Even they wouldn't come out; not in this.'

'Practical . . .' murmured Rowan, thinking of walking from her bedroom each morning and seeing a brick wall instead of miles and miles of valley and moors. 'Mum, listen to me. If you do this, it won't matter what happens next week. Because, if you do this, they've won. You'll be giving them your life. Our life. Mum . . .?'

Eleanor did not answer. Rowan stared at her unresponsive back and suddenly felt so tired that she wanted to curl up and sleep right there, in the splintered glass and cement dust. She moved up close to Eleanor without thinking about it, like a small child looking for safety, and they stood together, watching silently as the wind carved the drifts into glittering pillars and frozen waves of snow. Rowan forgot why she had run all the way home. Her wonderful idea had melted away and she had absolutely no idea what to do next.

She began to shiver in her wet clothes and Eleanor

looked at her properly for the first time since she had come in.

'Are you cold?' she said, and turned to touch Rowan's dripping hair. 'Oh, you're soaked through, sweetheart . . .'

'I – I've been walking,' said Rowan, pushing her head into Eleanor's hand and resting her cheek in the warm palm. The touch brought hope flooding back. For a few seconds, she almost believed that Eleanor would spring into action like she used to, helping her out of her wet clothes and bringing a towel to dry her with. Maybe she would even make hot chocolate and cinnamon toast and they could sit in front of the old stove together and forget about the last six months . . .

And she would have her mother back.

But then Eleanor turned away, her attention drifting to the window and the snow. Rowan came back to reality with a jolt. Her head cleared and, suddenly, she remembered what it was she had to do. Eleanor had lost her way. Eleanor was about to give up and lie down in the snow. It was up to Rowan to guide her back to the road. Back to their life.

But how to start? Rowan let her gaze sweep the room until she saw the new brick wall. She grinned fiercely, strode over to the clutter of tools the workmen had left, and hefted the largest sledgehammer in her hands.

Then setting her shoulders, Rowan squared up to the wall.

PART ONE

THE POWER OF NAMES

One

It was a still, hot evening in July when Rowan set fire to her school tie. She stuck a garden cane deep into the soil of the biggest geranium pot on the terrace, knotted the tie to the end of it and set to work with a box of matches. Bright sunshine outdid the flames, reducing them to a pale quiver so that the tie appeared to writhe on the end of the cane like a worm on a hook.

'Oh, weird! Do you see that, Mum? It looks as though it's moving by itself, like it's alive, a – a stripy snake or something . . .'

Eleanor did not answer. She was gazing at the burning tie in the same concentrated way that she would watch a film or read a book. She had the ability, rare in anyone over ten years old, to put her body on pause while her mind absorbed every detail of what was going on in front of her. Even her dark cloud of hair was motionless in the evening calm and there was only the slight flicker of a pulse at her throat to suggest that she would ever move again.

Rowan studied her mother, safe in the knowledge that Eleanor would not notice. She was tiny. Five foot two with delicate, bird bones. Like a little doll-person, thought Rowan. Except Eleanor was brown and angular, not pink and dimpled. And she wasn't stiff

7

and bland and lifeless like a doll, but full of a quick energy.

OK, forget the doll bit, thought Rowan. More like a scale model with all the working parts. People seemed to like it. They were fascinated by Eleanor's neat little frame in the same way that they were fascinated by miniature steam trains or wristwatch televisions or any of the pocket-sized, mail-order gadgets in the Sunday supplements.

Rowan, in contrast, was big-boned and fair, with the sort of healthy looks that sold yogurt and sun beds. As far as she could tell from the photographs, she was a duplicate of her father. Rowan sometimes wondered whether Eleanor minded looking at a clone of her ex-husband every day. He had even passed on his distinctive eyes; blue with a darker line circling the rim of the iris.

Eleanor's eyes were brown and so dark it was hard to make out the pupil at the centre. How can something be dark and bright at the same time, thought Rowan, seeing how Eleanor's eyes glittered as she stared at the tie. Some people found such intensity disconcerting. Luke, for instance. All his charm and easy wit seemed to vanish when he was confronted with one of Eleanor's stares.

'I wish she wouldn't look at me so hard when I'm talking to her,' he had said a few weeks earlier, after a particularly painful ten-minute wait for Rowan.

'She doesn't mean it,' Rowan had said, struggling to fasten her seat belt as he accelerated away from the barn. 'She's interested in you . . .'

'Yeah, like a lie detector's interested,' grumbled Luke, making her wonder, briefly, what he had to hide. 'It gets me so uptight when she does that. I completely dried up back there. Hell, I can see why your dad ran away to America, if she used to give him looks like that.'

That was the night of the row. The only row in their eight months together. It wasn't even a proper row, if a proper row was two people shouting. She had sucked in her breath as his words hit home and then yelled at him to stop the car. Five minutes later she was still yelling and he had turned into an ice sculpture. In the end she gave up and stormed back to the barn, leaving him staring straight ahead through the car windscreen, his face as white and hard as bone.

The next day, Luke turned up to take her to a party as though nothing had happened. Rowan got the message; forget the heavy stuff – keep the good times rolling. Mostly she was happy with that, but occasionally the unresolved fight came back to bother her, throbbing like a splinter that needed to come out.

Now Rowan shook the bad memory away and turned back to the burning tie. As she watched the loathed rhubarb and custard stripes turn black and crispy, the reality finally sank in: she had finished her last GCSE exam. A wave of delight washed over her and she began a hip-swinging dance around the tie, waving her arms above her head. 'No more uniform,' she crowed, 'no more Year Eleven, no more assemblies—'

'No more French verbs,' chanted Eleanor, falling into step behind Rowan. 'No more chemical symbols . . . please!'

Rowan giggled. Eleanor had spent hours testing her on her Chemistry. 'No more chemical symbols,' she repeated. 'No more—' Rowan stopped suddenly, causing Eleanor to cannon into the back of her.

'What? What's the matter?'

'—unless I fail.'

'Of course you won't!'

'Luke failed, the first time round.'

'I know, but he passed the next year when he

actually got down to a bit of work. Look at him now, he's halfway through his A levels and doing fine! You'll pass, sweetheart. You worked hard.'

'So did you, Mum. All that testing, and my favourite meals, and taking me off for walks on the moors when it got too much. Thanks. You were great.'

'Don't stop yet! Say some more nice things.'

'At least I'll never have to wear that horrible uniform again, even if I do end up with re-takes in the sixth form,' said Rowan, brightening. 'Go on, Mum, let's burn the rest of it.'

' "Now all the youth of England are on fire—" '

'Shut up, Mum. I've had enough of *Henry V* for a while.'

'You recognize it! I'm impressed. In my experience anything learned for an exam gets forgotten the minute it's over. Stupid system! Plus you end up with year after year of literature-haters—'

'Mum, you're changing the subject again.'

Eleanor grinned. 'Ah, yes. The burning issue. Can I just say – good school skirts cost a lot? And can I just say – Carol in my drama group has a daughter in Year Nine and not much money?'

'And can I just say – chocolate cake?' said Rowan.

Eleanor's head went up. She sniffed the air, turned and raced into the barn.

Rowan settled into the cushions of the old bentwood rocker and set up a gentle rhythm. As she rocked, she gazed at the view spread out in front of her. The barn was in an ideal position, high on a valley side and apparently surrounded by countryside. In fact Bickersford, the small town where Eleanor worked and Rowan went to school, was only a few minutes away, but it was tucked out of sight behind the barn, in the next valley.

The terrace was U-shaped and jutted out into a swathe of land owned by the farmer who had sold them the barn. The fields swept from the barn down the valley side, divided by low stone walls and hedges and dotted with trees. On windy spring days, when the young wheat rippled like a green sea, the terrace seemed to Rowan like the prow of a stone ship, riding the crest of a huge wave.

On the opposite side of the valley, the slope rose even higher than the barn, climbing up to meet the edge of the moors. The rich colours of crops and cow pastures on the lower slopes gradually faded into grey stone and heather, with white flecks of sheep and yellow flecks of gorse. That was where they had walked, she and Eleanor, between bouts of revision. If she screwed up her eyes, she could even pick out the outcrop where they had sat, reviving her oxygen-starved brain and putting exams into perspective.

Rowan smiled and closed her eyes. The flagstones were warm under her bare feet, gently releasing stored-up heat from the day's sun. Bees buzzed among the terracotta pots and baskets of flowers edging the terrace and the rich, dark smell of baking chocolate cake drifted from the barn behind her. The whole summer stretched ahead: weeks and weeks of long, lazy days with Luke and the gang. Perfect!

The crunching beside her left ear woke her up. She turned towards the noise, wrinkling her nose against the pungent smell of crushed geranium leaves, and opened her eyes to a close-up view of a set of teeth the size, shape and colour of old piano keys.

'Mum!' she yelled, shrinking back in the chair. 'Mum!'

The cows all jumped backwards away from the terrace and stood there, legs braced for a quick get-away, shaking their heads reproachfully. The nearest one still had an orange frill of geranium flowers around its mouth and a black frill of flies around its watery brown eyes.

11

'Yuk,' said Rowan, looking away. 'Why can't you just use eyeliner like the rest of us?' She glared at the next cow. The cow stared back, then stuck out its long, pink tongue and shoved it up first one wet nostril, then the other.

'Oh, yuk!' screamed Rowan, jumping to her feet and waving her arms around. 'Get lost, you disgusting cows. You're turning me off milk.'

The cows wheeled and galloped to the middle of the field, where they stood in a clump, staring mournfully. Eleanor laughed from the doorway behind her.

'You used to love having a herd of cows in your back garden. I remember coming out here once, when you were just two, and you were perched right on the edge of the terrace, surrounded by cows trying to eat your hair and your dungarees. I was horrified, all I could think of was you getting dragged down into the field with all those sharp, stamping hooves. No wall here then, you see. Your dad didn't want boundaries; he wanted it to be open, as though the barn was flowing out to the valley and the valley was flowing into the barn. Nice idea, but . . .' Eleanor shook her head, remembering.

'This wall was up three weeks later, though. I made sure of it. That was the one time I got my own way when we were converting this place.'

'Did you and Dad have a lot of fights about it?'

'Yes. Yes we did. The architect versus the mother. He wanted light and air, I wanted safety and storage space. He won, mostly. Two years in a caravan with a baby and no running water and you stop caring about the finer points; you just want the place to be finished so you can move in. We were in total harmony about the window, though,' added Eleanor, stepping out onto the terrace and turning to look up at the huge glass wall that had replaced the original barn doors.

12

'Did I fall, that time with the cows?' asked Rowan, watching the herd out of the corner of her eye as they sidled back to the terrace.

'No. I grabbed you away and you laughed up at me ... God, you were a sweet little thing. You even managed to look sweet drenched in cow slobber,' said Eleanor, gazing up at Rowan with a fond smile. Rowan squirmed. 'It only seems like yesterday, and now here I am, planning to go off and leave you. Are you sure you'll be all right here on your own?'

'Eleanor, I'm a big girl now,' said Rowan in her independent voice, but she couldn't help glancing in at the upper gallery of the barn and thinking of sleeping up there alone, with the moonlight stealing in through the great wall of glass.

'I'll cancel. I'll stay,' said Eleanor, catching the glance.

'Mum! Don't you dare! You've been a lecturer in that English Department for years and it's the first time you've been asked to do a residential. You deserve it. The college won't ask again, you know, if you let them down now. I'll be fine. I'm looking forward to it.'

Eleanor nodded, frowning. Then her face cleared. 'What am I worried about? It is the end of the month after all. Everyone knows it's chocolate cake weekend – you'll be swamped! Come on. I've just got time to help you ice it.'

'Hadn't you better pack, first?'

'What, throw a few clothes in a bag? Two minute job,' called Eleanor over her shoulder as she disappeared into the barn.

'Two hours, more like,' muttered Rowan, thinking of the mounds of clothes that grew in the darker corners of Eleanor's bedroom like multicoloured mushrooms. Then she shrugged her shoulders and headed for the kitchen.

* * *

'Of course, you could always just pop over the road to IQ's house to sleep,' said Eleanor, pouring the last of the melted chocolate over the cake. 'Margaret won't mind. She'd probably prefer it to having to keep checking on you.'

'Mum!'

'Look, I didn't ask her, honestly. I just said I was going to be away for the weekend.'

'Ah, but you knew she'd insist, didn't you? You know what Margaret's like. The Universal Mother. Do you remember when me and IQ were little and you and Margaret used to see us across the road to each other's houses when we wanted to play?'

'I remember.'

'Well, she still does it to me.'

'What! Oh, come on—'

'I swear, Margaret still sees me across the road when I leave their house! She'll pretend she's come out to weed the garden or put out the milk bottles, or something, but she's watching me across the road to the barn, I know she is. And now you've told her I'm on my own, she won't be able to leave me alone.'

'Sorry,' said Eleanor, without looking the slightest bit repentant. 'I know! You could have someone to stay over. My room'll be empty. Why don't you ask Sally or, um, Luke or Theresa—'

'Why do you always do that?'

'Do what?'

'That little "um" just before you say "Luke"?'

'Do I?'

'Yes! You can never just say Luke. It's always, um, Luke. A little pause. You don't think much of him, do you?'

'Well now Rowan, I wouldn't say that. He's a nice enough boy. I – well – to be honest sweetheart, I wonder whether he really likes you?'

'Of course he likes me – we've been going out

14

together for eight months, haven't we? That's a record for him.'

'Hmmm. He doesn't show it much, though, does he? I never see you holding hands or having a cuddle and, given the choice of seats, he always goes for our big armchair instead of next to you on the sofa.'

'Yes, well he's not like your drama lot, Mum. All luvvie and darling and flinging their arms around everyone.'

Eleanor let out her unlikely honk of a laugh, which always earned her startled looks from strangers, as though they had just heard a sparrow impersonate a goose. 'Oh, come on! They're not luvvies. They're just ordinary people learning how to let go a bit. Nothing wrong with self-expression, darling luvvie,' she cried, putting Rowan's head in an arm-lock and planting a kiss on her forehead.

'What I mean,' said Rowan, extricating herself from Eleanor's armpit, 'is Luke's not into public hand-holding and stuff like that. I think it's because of the way he's been brought up. His parents are so – so—'

'Cold? Snooty?'

'Formal. He's different when we're on our own.'

'Oh, good. He's very keen to get things right, isn't he? He gets quite anxious about it. Did you see how he was with that book of cartoons I was showing him the other day? It was as though I'd given him an exam paper. I wished I hadn't shown him, afterwards. I mean, I wanted him to enjoy them but all I did was make him worried in case he didn't get the joke. And sometimes I think going out with you might be another part of getting things right; getting life right. Passing the test, you know?'

Rowan was staring at Eleanor. 'No, I don't know.'

'OK. Well, you're one of the most popular girls in the school—'

'Eleanor!'

'No, listen, you are. You're very pretty and you're clever and you've got a good sense of style and you're confident – people like you, kiddo, so don't act all coy about it. And – sometimes I just think, um, Luke might see you as the right girl rather than the only girl, you know? Just like having the right car, the right clothes, the right image . . .'

Rowan began to giggle. 'Well, his parents don't think I'm the right girl. His parents think I'm a penniless pleb, only they're too genteel to say so.'

'But that's even the right sort of rebellion, isn't it?' mused Eleanor, leaning back against the bench and frowning at the ceiling. 'He's following an accepted tradition, kicking against his parents a bit . . . They're not too bothered. If they really wanted him to stop seeing you, they'd just threaten to take his car away—'

'Mum! Stop it! I only asked whether you liked him. Don't take him to bits like a – like a piece of bad literature – he's my boyfriend!' Rowan turned her back on Eleanor and began grating a slab of white chocolate with fierce, quick strokes.

Behind her, Eleanor closed her eyes, lifted an imaginary gun to her head and pulled the trigger. She was reaching out to touch Rowan's stiff shoulders when she spied the icing syringe full of whipped cream. Her eyes lit up and her hand changed direction.

Rowan was at the delicate stage of grating the last two centimetres of chocolate when Eleanor's shriek broke her concentration. She whirled round, sucking a grated fingertip. Eleanor had squirted a large blob of whipped cream on the end of her nose and stuck a cherry on top.

'Will you look at that?' she moaned.

'What?' said Rowan, trying not to smile.

'I always get an enormous pimple just when I need to make a good impression,' said Eleanor, crossing her eyes to look at the cherry. As they watched, the blob of cream began a slow slide down the slope of Eleanor's nose and, just as it seemed the whole mess would drop to the floor, she stuck out her tongue and caught it, whipping it into her mouth like a frog with a fly.

Rowan burst out laughing in spite of herself and Eleanor joined in.

'You made me grate my longest nail off,' said Rowan, when they had calmed down.

'Sorry,' said Eleanor, putting her arms around Rowan and squeezing hard. 'I'm sorry – all right?'

Rowan nodded and butted her head gently against her mother's. 'And I'm staying here on my own – all right?'

'All right. Come on, then. I'd better put the rest of this cream where it's supposed to go.'

Twenty minutes later, they stood back and assessed their creation.

'Do you think we've overdone it a bit this time?' asked Eleanor, doubtfully.

'It looks like a wedding hat,' spluttered Rowan.

'Cholesterol city! Well, everyone's so good about what they eat these days – we've got to have a treat once in a while. Perhaps I should've made two cakes – one to take with me to the residential. On second thoughts, most of the women in Jeff Mason's Theatre Group are permanent members of the Thursday Slimming Group too. I know, because my drama lot go and make fun of them through the Sports Hall windows after class.'

'Mum!'

'I said they do it, not me.'

17

'Still, I don't think you're going to fit in exactly on this weekend.'

'No, I'm not, am I,' frowned Eleanor, taking the remark seriously. 'I can't imagine Jeff Mason's group being happy with my improvisation exercises. They like a script to follow; the blander the better. They're into performance, not discovery. And Jeff Mason thinks impro's a load of rubbish. I know that for a fact – he's told me often enough, especially since he was made Head of Department.'

'Why did he ask you along, then?'

Eleanor sighed. 'He didn't actually come up and ask me. You know he hasn't really spoken to me since I went over his head that time he tried to cut one of my courses. What he did was to send a memo inviting me. Then, when I phoned him to say thanks, he was really quite rude and hostile. I think asking me on the course is his way of calling a truce and I think he was embarrassed, so I let him get away with it.'

'Do you want to go?'

Eleanor made a face. 'Well, it's meant to be a lovely place, this conference centre. It's a big old hall, right out in the country, with beautiful grounds, tennis courts, a swimming pool ... Some people in the department have been trying to get in on these week-ends for years.'

'But do you want to go?'

Eleanor made an even worse face. 'Not really. As you said, I don't fit in. That group, that whole scene – I'm just not interested. I don't like the way they've made their Theatre Group into an exclusive club. The courses at the college are meant to be for everyone, but that Theatre Group, if someone they don't want tries to join, somehow it's always full. And it's not just the Theatre Group. They're all in the Tennis Club, the Golf Club and just about every committee and body of governors you can think of. They've been running the whole town between them for years. Jeff Mason too. He loves that sort of thing. And of course all the women flirt with him—'

'Oh, yuk! Not oily Jeff Mason. That is gross,' said Rowan.

'No, really, a lot of people think he's good-looking, in a B-film sort of way. Anyway, he's never turned on the charm for us two. You should see what he's like with these women – he undergoes a complete personality change.' Eleanor shuddered.

'So, why are you going, Mum? It's not like you, to do something you don't want to do.'

'Because I appreciate the invitation. I didn't think he had it in him, to make the first move, back down, whatever you want to call it. Everyone says he's the enemy-for-life type. It didn't bother me socially, but I'd sort of resigned myself to being out in the career wilderness at the college.

'So, I'll be there, ready to get stuck in, at seven o'clock tonight—'

'What time?'

'Coffee and registration at seven,' said Eleanor, following Rowan's gaze to the kitchen clock. 'Oh no! It can't be that time! I should've left ten minutes ago.'

Rowan stood at the kitchen door waving as Eleanor's dirty green Citroen rattled down the hill. She waited, staring down the empty road, even after the car had disappeared round the big bend into town. Eleanor had already reversed back up the hill once, with the little car whining all the way, because she had forgotten to kiss Rowan goodbye.

This time the road stayed empty. Rowan leaned back against the warm stone wall of the barn, relishing the silence which flooded in to fill the vacuum left by Eleanor's noisy departure. Her eye was caught by a flutter of movement at the window of one of the terraced houses across the road. IQ's mum was standing at her kitchen window holding up a teapot and beckoning her over. Rowan groaned through her teeth as she fixed her face in a smile. She waved back, deliberately misunderstanding, then ducked into the barn, pretending not to notice Margaret waving the teapot above her head and banging on the glass.

Rowan locked the door and, after a moment's thought, slid the bolts across too. Then she turned and looked around the empty kitchen. It felt different, being alone in the barn for a whole weekend. She had often whiled away a few hours on her own when Eleanor was at the college, but this was too big a stretch of time to be bridged by simply waiting. Rowan grinned and hugged herself as a sudden excitement curled up her spine and made her scalp tingle. The barn was hers for two nights and two days. Rowan was in charge.

Two

The doorbell rang fifty seconds after Rowan opened her curtains the next morning. She made a grab for her dressing-gown and pulled it on, frowning into her bedroom mirror. It was a little too early for visitors, even on a chocolate cake Saturday. She picked up her hairbrush then flung it down again and hurried to the window instead. The visitor at the kitchen door was hidden by the sloping porch roof even when she squashed her cheek against the glass and closed one eye. As Rowan hovered, biting her lip, the sun came out from behind a cloud and a long, lanky shadow appeared, stretching from the kitchen door, right across the grass and into the road.

Rowan grinned and headed for the stairs.

IQ gave her one sharp, assessing look when she opened the door. Then, apparently satisfied, he ducked under the door frame into the kitchen. He headed for the fridge and folded himself up like a pocket ruler until his head was low enough to look inside.

'See?' Rowan said. 'I'm still breathing. Nothing got me in the night. You can go back to Margaret and put in your report. Yes, Rowan slept well. No, she's not missing her mum. And, no, she doesn't want to come over for breakfast.'

'You didn't sleep well,' said IQ comfortably, emerging from the fridge with the chocolate cake. 'Your eyes are all pink and squinty.'

Rowan turned to look at herself in the kitchen mirror. He was right; it had been a bad night. The barn had been full of creaks and rustlings as it settled around her after the day's heat. She must have spent her life ignoring those same noises, but last night she couldn't stop listening; compulsively identifying each one. That gurgling under her bed was the pipes in the bathroom below. That click which sounded just like someone releasing the safety catch on a revolver was the television cooling down. She had lain awake for hours, wide-eyed in the dark, with the duvet pulled up to her chin and her body poker-straight beneath it. There was light behind the curtains when she finally edged into a skinny, stunted apology of a sleep.

'OK, I didn't sleep well, but only because it was my first night on my own, ever. I'll be fine tonight, now I've done it once. Don't you tell Margaret I didn't sleep. She'll frog-march me over the road to stay at your house.'

'I know how to handle mum,' said IQ, cutting a huge slice of cake.

Rowan turned back to the mirror and prodded the puffy skin under her eyes. 'Oh, no,' she moaned. 'Luke's coming over today and I look like a bloodhound.'

'Cold tea bags,' said IQ, promptly. 'Put them on your eyes and lie down for ten minutes. Mum swears by them.'

'I haven't got any cold tea bags.'

'Ah, but you will if you make us a pot, won't you?' he grinned.

'I walked into that one,' said Rowan, reaching for the cupboard where the tea bags were kept. The handle came off in her hand and she laid it on the

22

bench with a sigh. 'I cannot believe that still catches me out, after all this time.'

' "I'll get that fixed next month, sweetheart, when we've got a bit of spare cash," ' mimicked IQ, managing to capture the essence of Eleanor despite his deep voice and great height.

'That and five hundred other repair jobs,' giggled Rowan, prising open the cupboard door with the bread knife. 'She's dreadful. She spends it all on books and concerts and trips to the theatre. The barn could be falling down around her ears and she'd still insist on taking me to see some wonderful new production she's heard about.'

'I think it's great,' said IQ. 'I think she's great. And I think y . . . I think . . .'

Rowan looked up. IQ was staring at her with unusual intensity. 'What? What do you think?'

'. . . I think – I think I'll have another slice,' said IQ, turning away from Rowan and reaching for the cake.

They took the tea through to Rowan's favourite room at the front of the barn. Whereas the back half of the barn was like a normal house with a bathroom and a kitchen downstairs and two bedrooms above, the whole of the front had been left as one spectacular space. It was two storeys high and flooded with light from the wall of glass that looked out over the terrace and the valley beyond.

They sat in companionable silence drinking their tea and watching cloud shadows slide down the valley slopes. The windows were flawless and so clean it seemed there was nothing to stop them walking right out into the fields. Eleanor might rate housework on a par with train-spotting in her list of useless activities, but she always kept the terrace windows clean.

23

'You see, there's a point to this sort of cleaning,' she would say, climbing the stepladders with a long-handled sponge in her hand. 'It's not just cleaning for cleaning's sake. We get light, we get space. We get the whole valley in our front room!'

IQ drained his mug and pushed his glasses up to the bridge of his nose with his middle finger. 'I'll just, um, have a look,' he said, unfolding himself from the depths of the sofa. Rowan rolled her eyes.

'As long as you don't show me, OK?'

'OK,' he agreed, beginning to search through Eleanor's books with an avid look on his face. The books were everywhere. They had long ago over-flowed the bookcases and were piled up in towers around the room. Every tread of the open plan stair-case was stacked with them and a low wall had grown along the edge of the upper gallery, stopping on a level with the top of the railing, for safety's sake.

These book constructions looked permanent enough but they underwent a process of constant change. Every so often, usually in the middle of the night, Eleanor surged through them like a wind through sand dunes, shifting and sifting; searching for some half-remembered lines. Rowan's sleep would be invaded by sighings and mutterings and the papery riffle of disturbed pages and the next morning she would walk out of her bedroom into a changed land-scape. Sometimes she would find the book that Eleanor had uncovered during the night lying open outside her door like a shell on a beach.

Half-remembered lines were of no interest to IQ. He was looking behind the stacks of books and peer-ing down inside their spines. He was hunting for spiders.

'As if you didn't have a shed full of them already,' said Rowan. 'Honestly, anything small and hairy, with more legs than nature intended and you're lost. When are you going to grow out of spiders?'

They both knew it wasn't a serious question. IQ had been fascinated by spiders and insects for as long as Rowan could remember. By the time he was ten, he knew so much about his favourite creatures that everyone had started calling him IQ, even though he insisted it was more to do with interest than intelligence. When they were younger, she and IQ had gone on collecting expeditions together but, at some point, spiders had lost their appeal for Rowan. She didn't exactly dislike them; she just wasn't interested any more.

'Eight legs are perfectly natural, for a spider,' murmured IQ, carefully lifting aside Eleanor's collection of Celtic folk tales. Rowan smiled, remembering the first time he had shown an interest in the books. Eleanor had been thrilled to find him going through her stack of Thomas Hardy novels.

'Oh, IQ,' she cried, thinking she had found a ten year old literature-lover. 'I didn't know you liked that sort of book.'

'The old ones are the best,' said IQ.

Eleanor's smile of agreement faded as she watched him shake *The Mayor of Casterbridge* until a fat black spider dropped out of the spine into his hand.

'See?' he said. 'Great habitat.'

Eleanor still had a good laugh about that one. 'Great habitat,' she would splutter, if Rowan pointed out the thick layer of dust collecting on some of the book piles.

Rowan watched IQ's careful search for a moment more, then she fished the used tea bags from the pot and headed for her room.

Theresa was the next to arrive.

'You look glittery,' said Rowan, opening the door.

'Glittery?' said Theresa, raising an eyebrow.

'Um. Did I say glittery? Wrong word. I meant good. You look good.'

But 'glittery' was exactly the right word. Theresa's hair glinted like filaments of burnished copper as she bounced into the sunlit main room of the barn. She was wearing a shimmering summer dress, green with silver threads running through the material, and her skin was covered with a glistening coating of tanning lotion. Even her eyes glittered as she sent searching glances around the room.

Rowan saw the glances. 'Luke isn't here yet,' she said, without thinking.

'Oh,' sighed Theresa, and glittered a little less.

An instant later, she faced Rowan with a flash of guilty anger as she realized what she might have given away.

Now why did I say that, thought Rowan, staring back. So she fancies Luke. Her and half the school. There was no need to let her know I know, especially since she's been so friendly these last few months.

For one second, two, they stood silently, eyes locked, while Rowan tried to think of a way to set things right.

'Oops,' came a wry voice from the gallery, and the spell was broken.

'IQ's here, though,' continued Rowan, as though nothing had happened.

Theresa's expression smoothed out like icing under a knife. 'Hi, IQ!' she trilled, turning away from Rowan and dancing backwards to look up at the gallery. 'No more exams. Isn't it great?'

IQ looked down at Theresa. The round lenses of his glasses reflected the sunlight like two small moons, hiding the expression in his eyes.

'Yeah,' he said. 'Great. Now you can concentrate on – other things.'

'Too right. I'm going to enjoy myself this summer. Starting now.' Theresa whirled across the room to the terrace doors and flung them open. 'Look at that sunshine! I don't know how you two can skulk around indoors on a day like this. Come on! We need chairs, drinks, music . . .'

Rowan laughed. That was what she liked about Theresa. Things happened when she was around.

The terrace was bathed in a drowsy heat and they floated in it, enjoying a pointless, lazy debate over who was the most sadistic teacher in the school. Rowan was making the case for Eva Conrad, the Home Economics teacher.

'Conrad the Barbarian. She's got to be the worst. She runs that kitchen like an army camp. Little Gary Armstrong used to wipe up the hob while he was still stirring his sauce, he was so scared of her catching him with a dirty work surface.'

'That must've been difficult,' said IQ. 'Like patting your head and rubbing your stomach at the same time.' He tried to demonstrate but could only either rub or pat, not both together. 'See. Told you it was difficult.'

'No, it's easy,' said Rowan. 'You have to get the rubbing going first . . . And then add the patting . . . There!'

IQ began to shake with laughter.

'What's the matter? I'm doing it, aren't I?'

'Yeah, but the hand you're patting with is whizzing round in these crazy little circles. You look like you've just lost your hat – or your hair . . .' He collapsed in giggles again.

'Oh, anyway,' said Rowan, giving up. 'What about

27

the week Conrad made us all come in and clean the cookers every lunchtime?'

'Yeah, but someone did crack a raw egg into her handbag, so she had a reason for making us suffer. Now, a sadistic teacher makes you suffer to give him pleasure, like Test-tube Bayley. What about that Chemistry experiment with the stinking sulphur gas, when he made us—'

'Ice!' cried Theresa, jumping to her feet. 'We need more ice.'

'She's looking after us this morning,' smiled Rowan, watching Theresa rush through to the kitchen.

'Oh, it's not ice she's after,' said IQ.

'What?'

IQ leaned forward, pushed his glasses up to the bridge of his long nose and stared at Rowan. His eyes were hazel, which meant that they were a changeable mixture of green, blue and grey. For now, Rowan noticed, they were the same stony green as Eleanor's jade earrings.

'Theresa could see the Bickersford road from her seat,' he said.

'So?' said Rowan.

'So she could see all the cars coming up the hill from the town.'

'So?' said Rowan, again.

IQ raked the hair back from his forehead but, being straight and silky-fine, it immediately flopped back again. 'Why do you always think everyone's so nice?' he hissed.

Rowan stared, astonished, until he shook his head and smiled, his eyes changing to a soft grey-green.

'Doesn't matter,' he sighed.

'Look who was at the door,' called Theresa, coming out onto the terrace with her arm hooked through Luke's.

'What a surprise,' murmured IQ, but Rowan was jumping up from her chair and didn't hear.

'Hi,' she smiled, enjoying her first look at him.

'Hello, youngsters,' grinned Luke, carelessly swinging his car keys. 'All your little exams over? If you think that was tough, wait until September. You won't know what's hit you. GCSE's are a doddle compared to 'A' levels.'

'Are they?' said IQ, who had spent the past two months trapped within ramparts of revision notes. 'Are they really? I suppose you would know all about GCSE exams, wouldn't you, Luke? The voice of experience talking there.'

Luke gave him a suspicious glance. IQ stared back, innocently. Luke rescued his slipping grin but Rowan could see a muscle beginning to twitch on the side of his jaw. She knew he was trying to work out whether IQ was laughing at him; Luke did not tolerate being laughed at, unless he had planned it that way.

' "The voice of experience"?' sneered Luke, behind his grin. 'What do you mean?'

Theresa giggled but Rowan was silent, giving IQ an irritated stare. What was it with him, recently? It was not the first time he had challenged Luke. Tensions had grown between them that she preferred to ignore.

'I mean you did your GCSE's twice, so you must know what you're talking about.' IQ gave Luke a smile which showed all his teeth but his eyes were the blunt grey of lead shot. Luke grinned back, his hands slowly curling into fists.

'Come on,' said Rowan, just to break the thickening silence. She stopped, at a loss what to say next, and turned to Theresa for help but Theresa was watching the boys with a hungry glitter in her eyes.

'Come on,' echoed Rowan and dried up again, blushing angrily at her sudden dumbness. Luke gave no sign of hearing but IQ turned his head and looked at her.

She bit her lip.

IQ took a deep breath. 'Speaking of September,' he said, clambering to his feet and standing beside Luke. 'What about us two teaming up?'

Luke turned towards him, frowning, and IQ turned too, bending his knees so that they were face to face. His nose looked cartoonishly long, positioned a centimetre from Luke's perfect Roman profile.

'I mean, just look at us. We're both so devastatingly handsome and stylish, if we work together we'll be irresistible. The girls will fall at our feet.'

IQ turned back to Rowan and Theresa. 'Won't you?' he said, putting his arm around Luke's shoulder and striking a pose. He was twenty centimetres taller than Luke and skinny with it. His silky brown hair fell straight from a centre parting to his shoulders, making him look very much like a long-handled mop.

'Well, go on then,' he said, clamping his knees together and turning his long feet out sideways. 'Fall. Fall!'

Theresa and Rowan looked down at IQ's feet, which were encased in a pair of weird-looking green sandals with domed fronts like dodgem cars. They both gazed at the sandals for a few seconds then looked sideways. As soon as their eyes met, they collapsed into fits of laughter and sank to the ground, clutching at one another.

'See?' said IQ. 'They fell. What a team we'd make. How about it, Luke, baby?'

'Get lost,' said Luke, grinning confidently again.

'I understand. I'm just too much for you, aren't I?'

'That's one way of putting it,' said Luke, heading for the nearest chair.

Theresa leapt to her feet. 'Not there! Over here.' She guided Luke to the lounger where she had been

30

sitting. 'See,' she said, plumping the cushions and pointing to a cold drink waiting in the shade of the terrace wall. 'We're all ready for you. Except for Rowan, who hasn't even changed out of her night things. Still, I suppose you're used to her slobbish behaviour by now.' Theresa threw Rowan a fond, only-joking smile.

Rowan looked down at her sloppy joe T-shirt and baggy shorts. 'These aren't my night things.'

'Oh. Sorry Rowan, it's just, they look as though you slept in them, you see. That's why when I got here earlier, I thought you and IQ had just got up . . .'

'Just got up?' Rowan giggled. 'Theresa, IQ didn't stay here, did you?' She looked at IQ, but he was busy studying Theresa as though she was a particularly interesting insect.

'Mind you,' said Rowan. 'Eleanor did suggest it. She also suggested you and Luke and Sally . . . But I told her I was too old to need a babysitter, so she's having to content herself with regular bulletins. She phoned last night to see if I was all right, and she phoned this morning. She'll probably phone tomorrow morning too.'

'God, don't parents hassle you?' sighed Theresa.

Rowan looked at her in surprise. 'I think it's sweet,' she said.

'Eleanor said I could stay?' asked Luke, frowning.

'Oh, she was just having a last minute guilt-trip about leaving me on my own—'

'I would've stayed.'

Rowan smiled and walked over to him. She wrapped her arms around his neck and put her lips to his ear. 'And what would your mum and dad've said about that?' she whispered, so that only Luke could hear.

Luke relaxed against her. 'They wouldn't've minded,' he whispered back.

31

'Are you crazy? They would rather roast you on a spit over their state-of-the-art barbecue pit than let you spend a night here.'

They leaned their heads together, shoulders shaking with laughter, and IQ watched them with rueful satisfaction.

'Nice try,' he said to Theresa, but she was crouched with her head down, going through a pile of CDs, and did not seem to hear.

IQ sat in Rowan's rocking chair, lifted his feet and stared at the green sandals. He waggled them about, did a Charlie Chaplin walk, then turned both his ankles inwards and clapped the soles together. Finally, he shouldered an imaginary rifle, aimed and fired. The sandals jumped in mid-air, shuddered and fell to the ground.

'Make my day, pumps,' he growled, and fell back, sniggering at his own joke. The combined scent of Rowan's camomile shampoo and apricot soap rose from the cushion behind his head and filled his nose. He gave a muffled groan and closed his eyes, letting his arms flop over the sides of the chair.

And something grabbed his wrist.

He gave a hoarse yell as the rocker was tipped backwards and held, poised, over the edge of the terrace wall.

'If you've scoffed all the cake, you're going to end up head first down here in this cow pat,' threatened a voice behind him.

'Sally!' gasped IQ, his nerve endings still fizzing with shock. 'Where did you come from?'

'Over the field fence. After leaning on the doorbell for five minutes without getting any answer. Now, how many slices?'

'Let me up, will you?'

The chair tipped further back. 'How many slices?'

'Two! Two.'

'Big or small?'

'Small.'

The chair tipped so far back, he began to slide out of it, upside down. 'Big! Huge! Enormous! Let me down!'

'OK.'

IQ yelled again as the chair shot forward on its rockers and catapulted him to his feet.

'You sure know how to get a guy excited, Sally Rylance,' he said, turning to look down at the small, dark face beaming up at him from the field.

'So that's why your knees are trembling. I thought it was fear. Here, grab a hold of this.' She hoisted a supermarket carrier bag over the terrace wall and he staggered as he caught it.

'The bosses are selling off mystery tins again,' said Sally, swinging herself up onto the terrace in one smooth move. 'Ten pence each. They're so good to their staff, aren't they?' She yanked her supermarket overall from the top of the bag, spread it out on the terrace and piled the tins on top of it. They glinted in the sunshine, with only the dotted lines of solidified glue to show that they had ever had labels. Sally fished a black marker pen from the pocket of her overall and sat cross-legged in front of the pile.

'Sorry about the door,' said Rowan, coming to sit opposite Sally. 'I didn't know when to expect you. Have you finished for the day?'

Sally shook her head. 'Split shift. I've got to be back at four. They'd better not put me on moving trolleys again,' she growled, pressing the raised bruises on each shin bone. 'Anyway, the good news is, I've got loads of extra work this summer, covering for staff holidays, so the expedition fund is really going to grow.'

'Brilliant!' said Rowan. 'I'll see whether old Tracy will give me some extra hours at the newsagent's this summer. And Dad'll probably send me another cheque if I pass my GCSE's. And one for my birthday . . .'

They beamed at one another, their shared dream hovering in the air between them.

'Peru first,' breathed Rowan.

'No, Kashmir,' said Sally.

'Inca gold, ancient cities, bottomless lakes—'

'Houseboats, mountains, maharajas' palaces—'

'Africa, then.'

'China.'

'The Gold Coast.'

'The Great Wall—'

'Oh, please,' begged Theresa. 'Why don't the pair of you just book a package deal to the Costa and get it out of your systems?'

They both turned to give Theresa a pitying look. Two weeks in a hotter version of Blackpool was not what they wanted. They were going to be travellers, not tourists. It was a life-time ambition and it was how they had become friends, back in Year Five. Rowan's first glimpse of Sally had been over the top of the newest *National Geographic* in the school library. She could still picture Sally's dark, intense little face glaring at her as they pulled the magazine back and forth between them. The fight had reached the hair-pulling stage when Miss Stubbs found them and told them if they couldn't share, then they couldn't look. So they had shared, and gradually the elbowing and page-hogging stopped as the colour photographs drew them in and took them to festivals in Mexico and underground houses in the Sahara Desert. Miss Stubbs wisely ignored the no-talking rule and, by the end of that lunchtime, Rowan and Sally were firm friends.

'Come on, then,' said Sally, turning her attention back to the pile of tins. 'Gather round. Hurry up, useless. You can pick out the beluga caviar.'

34

'The really good stuff doesn't come in tins, pleb,' said Luke, mildly, strolling over to join them. He put up with Sally's insults. Everybody did. Somehow Sally's insults didn't hurt because she delivered them with such affection.

'Steamed pudding,' said Theresa, plucking a tin from the pile.

'That's an easy one,' said Luke. 'You can tell by the shape of the tin. Like this one. Sardines!' He handed it to Sally, who wrote the contents on the side with her marker pen. They managed to name half the pile between them before they sat back to watch Sally sort out the rest. She had become an expert since she started her Saturday job at the supermarket. She weighed each tin in her hand, then put it to her ear and tipped it back and forth, listening carefully.

'Now this one's got a fair amount of liquid in it, and it's thick stuff—'

'Soup?' guessed IQ.

'Nope. Not sloppy enough. It moves too slowly. Baked beans, I reckon. And this one's pears . . . and that's, um . . . tuna. In brine,' she added with a boastful grin.

Only one tin gave her trouble. She hefted it, turned it, pressed the top and eventually shook her head. 'Well – someone in my family's in for a treat. Only trouble is, it might be the dog. This is either red salmon or Pedigree Chum. There.' She sat back to admire the neat stack of tins. 'Mum'll be pleased. I've got a couple of split bags too – some new kid in the unloading bay tried to slice open a box of plain flour with a stanley knife. And I've got first refusal on a cream cake if it's not sold by eight. The kids love cream cake.'

They were silent for a moment, looking at the tins. Rowan was thinking about Sally's chaotic family, all crammed into one house on Bickersford's Greenlaw estate. She thought about sharing a small bedroom with two sisters as Sally did. She thought about trying to revise for her GCSE's on a top bunk, surrounded by music and squabbles. She tried to imagine how she would cope with taking pot-luck from tins without labels, or sieving split bags of flour and sugar into empty, catering size ice-cream tubs. She wondered whether she would ever want to make a cake if it meant using cracked eggs and margarine past its sell-by date, then switching off everything else in the house to make sure the money in the meter lasted long enough to bake it. All these things she had seen in Sally's house at one time or another. Rowan couldn't decide which she would hate most; the lack of space or the lack of money.

IQ broke the silence. 'Speaking of cream cake . . .' he said, and everyone roared.

In bed that night, Rowan smiled, remembering IQ's look of wounded innocence. He had got his third slice of cake, and a huge helping of the spaghetti they had cooked up together for lunch. Her smile faded for a moment as she remembered the mess waiting to be cleared up in the kitchen, but she put it out of her mind and thought about the evening instead. Luke had driven to Bickersford to hire a video after the others left. They had curled up on the sofa together, but they hadn't watched much of the film. Rowan smiled again as she thought of how they had held one another on the doorstep at the end of the evening, not wanting to let go. She was still smiling when she fell asleep.

A full moon was framed in the doorway when Rowan jumped awake. She turned her head on the pillow and saw it, floating high above the terrace and shining in through the wall of glass. Pale light filtered between the gallery railings, striping the floor outside her room with lines of shadow and silver, like a barcode. She frowned and pushed up on one elbow. There had been a noise; a noise which didn't fit . . . She held still, listening, but the house was silent.

Rowan smacked herself on the forehead. 'Don't start that again,' she hissed and turned over, closing her eyes in a determined manner. That was when she heard the outside door closing, very softly. Her eyes flew open and her heart began to beat so hard and fast, it almost hurt.

Impossible, she thought. No one can get through there. Not with that big lock and the bolts and the chain . . . She stopped and closed her eyes, suddenly faced with a clear image of herself saying goodnight to Luke. She had shut the door, groaned at the state of the kitchen and – walked away. The lock, the bolts and the chain were useless because she had left them undone.

Terror swamped her. A thin, cold film of sweat coated her body and she shivered violently in her warm bed.

Phone! I need a phone, she thought. But the only phone in the house was on the kitchen wall and that was where the . . .

Rowan eased into a sitting position and strained towards the gallery, listening. The door between the kitchen and the main room clicked open. There was a soft thud as something heavy was dropped onto the sofa, then the pad of feet crossing the wooden floor. Whoever it was, they did not want to be heard. They had removed their shoes.

Rowan's mind raced.

. . . O God, please don't come upstairs if he comes upstairs I've got to hide in my wardrobe and he'll think the house is empty and take what he wants and go please go . . .

The first stair creaked. Rowan forgot all about the wardrobe and dived beneath the duvet. The feet padded up a few more stairs and stopped. Rowan made herself as flat and still as possible. Even with her head covered, she could hear someone breathing out there; a trembling, uneven rasping sound. She bit on a mouthful of duvet, fighting the desire to erupt from the bed, screaming. At last the feet turned and padded downstairs again. She heard the creak of the bottom step, then the bathroom door opening. The intruder was just below her now.

Rowan climbed from the bed on shaky legs, tiptoed across to her door and stood behind it. If she could somehow get past the bathroom, she could make a run for the outside door and get across the road to IQ's house. A sound from the bathroom gave her the courage to peer out at the gallery but all she could see was a moonlit blur. She realized that her eyes were full of tears and blinked to clear them. The gallery was empty as far as she could see. She took a step forward, and froze.

What if there were two of them?

Rowan stood, unable to move, imagining a figure with his back pressed against the wall outside her room, waiting to grab her as soon as she stepped out. She stood until her lungs were bursting and the breath she was holding came out in an explosive gasp. Nothing happened. No hands came round the corner to grab her. The gallery remained quiet and still.

Rowan took another breath and stepped through the door, every centimetre of skin cringing. Her eyes were rabbit-huge as she spun round in a high-speed check of the whole of the gallery.

Empty.

Eleanor's bedroom was dark and quiet. For a few

seconds Rowan stared in, wishing her mother was there to shake awake. Then she turned away, crept to the gallery rail and peered down into the main room. Silvery moonlight mingled with a faint blush of warmer light seeping from the bathroom and touched the edges of a black lump on the sofa. Rowan screwed up her eyes and picked out handles at the top of the shape. It was a large bag.

Then a bizarre sound carried upstairs – the rushing gush of fast-flowing water. The intruder was running a bath. Rowan began to shake her head in a dazed manner, then her eyes widened as a thought struck her. She crept back to her room, lifted the curtain and looked out of her open window at the road. Eleanor's green car was parked on the grass verge like an over-sized cricket, clicking softly as the engine cooled.

'Mother,' groaned Rowan. She should have guessed who it was as soon as the footsteps stopped halfway up the stairs. Eleanor always used to check on her like that, peering through the gallery rails to make sure she was in her bed. Rowan let her head drop to rest against the cool sill and stayed there for a time, weak with relief, letting the breeze dry the sweat on the back of her neck. When her legs had stopped shaking, she walked over to her bedside table and squinted at the luminous hands of her alarm clock.

'Two o'clock in the morning! I don't believe it—' Rowan headed downstairs to demand an explanation.

The crying stopped her dead, just outside the bath-room door. She had heard Eleanor cry before, but never like this. All the hairs along her spine rose in a shivering line as she listened to the monotonous, shuddering moans that were twisting out of her mother. They had a raw, throaty edge to them, as though she had cried for the whole of the long drive home, only stopping for the time it took to creep up the stairs and check on Rowan.

Rowan felt sick. She didn't want to see what was behind the bathroom door, but she made herself step forward. The room was full of steam. The water must be scalding to make so much steam on a hot summer night. Eleanor was sitting in the bath with her back to the door and Rowan could see that her skin below the water line was an angry pink. There were four bright new bruises circling each upper arm like an officer's stripes.

Rowan moved further into the room. Eleanor was washing her face with sharp, repetitive strokes. No, it was just her mouth. Rowan took another step forward. She was rubbing at her mouth with a . . . with a—

'Mum! What are you doing?'

Eleanor whirled round with the nail brush still clutched in one hand. Her lips and the skin around them were red and swollen from the scrubbing, but the rest of her face was deathly pale. Her black hair was plastered to her head and a thin line of blood trickled from a split in her lower lip.

Red as blood, white as snow, black as a crow's wing, thought Rowan, stupidly. Snow White. She shook the words away but they came back, beating in her head and making it hard to think.

'What's happened?' she asked and Eleanor gave a gasp and crossed her arms to hide her breasts. Eleanor, who often wandered naked from bedroom to bathroom with a book open in one hand and her robe trailing from the other, was crossing her arms to hide her breasts. The action filled Rowan with dread.

'Mum?' she said, and her voice came out high and shaky, like a little girl's.

Eleanor licked the blood from her lower lip and turned her back. 'You go to bed. Let me have my bath. I'll – see you in the morning,' she said, in a voice that strained to be normal.

'But, Mum—'

'Go – let me—'

'Please, Mum—'

Eleanor's voice splintered. 'Go to bed! Get out and leave me alone!'

Three

It was all wrong.

It looked like a normal, Sunday morning kitchen but, as Rowan stood at the door looking in, she was reminded of a horror story she had read about a man who woke from a strange dream of lights and flying to find himself in a hospital room where nothing was quite right. The flowers had no scent and the books on the bedside table were full of blank pages. The sink lacked a plughole and the framed mirror above it held a photograph of the opposite wall instead of a reflection. Even the friendly young doctor who came in to examine him was flawed, although the man didn't spot it until she tried to listen to his heart. He looked at the stethoscope and saw that it was part of her. Two ropes of flesh grew from her ears, merged under her chin, and ended in the warm sucker that was nuzzling his chest. The man ran screaming from the room and fell into the vast, silver depths of an alien spacecraft.

Rowan shuddered. The scene in the kitchen was like that hospital room. It felt wrong, as though it had been put together by some alien being with an imperfect understanding of how life worked in the barn. For a start, it was too early for Eleanor to be in the kitchen; she never got out of bed before ten o'clock on a Sunday morning. The silence was wrong too. Eleanor always switched on the radio as soon as she walked in, unless she had someone to talk to.

Then there was the top. The long-sleeved, sugar-pink, polo-necked top which Eleanor never wore because she said it made her look like a stick of rock. Hiding the bruises, thought Rowan, imagining how the four bright stripes on each arm must have darkened and purpled through the night. She's wearing it to hide those bruises. The ones that look as though someone grabbed her and dug their fingers into her arms and . . .

No. Not my mum.

Rowan's mind skittered away in panic, as it had done for hours and hours through the night, before she slept. She was afraid to give it a name, this thing that had happened to Eleanor. A name had power. To name this thing, even in her head, would be to define it, and then it would change from a blurred, grey shadow to a focused, solid shape that could not be ignored. That was why, when Eleanor finally left the bathroom and came to stand for a moment at the bottom of her bed, Rowan had closed her eyes and imitated sleep. And that was why she was hovering outside the kitchen now, testing the air. She dreaded the thought of Eleanor turning to her in tears, and saying she'd been—

No! Not my mum!

Rowan rushed into the kitchen, galvanized by the desire to get away from her thoughts. Eleanor was clearing up the debris from the spaghetti meal, which made Rowan very uneasy. It was an unwritten rule in the barn that they were each responsible for their own messes. She bit her lip and wondered what to say. That felt wrong, too. Speaking to Eleanor had never needed thinking about before; it had always been as natural as breathing.

43

'Morning,' she said, more brightly than she meant to.

Eleanor jumped. 'Hello,' she muttered, and went back to scraping strands of spaghetti from the wall.

'Sorry about that,' breezed Rowan, waving a shaky hand at the spaghetti. 'Luke said if it stuck to the wall it was done, so we were testing it out.'

'I see,' said Eleanor. There was a short silence, which Rowan jumped to fill.

'Look, you shouldn't be doing that, anyway. Leave it to me, OK? It's my mess. You finish your breakfast.'

Eleanor turned and frowned at the bowl of soggy cornflakes on the kitchen table as though she could not imagine how it had got there. She was pale, apart from her mouth, which looked red and sore. The silence crept in again and Rowan drove it out by whistling through her teeth as she gathered up the cold spaghetti and dumped it into a pan of congealed tomato sauce. Grabbing a spoon, she flipped open the lid of the kitchen bin and scraped and whistled without really looking at what she was doing. The last clotted lump of red sauce fell onto the green velvet and she turned away from the bin and stopped whistling.

Green velvet?

'Mum!' she said, forgetting to be careful. 'What's your dress doing in the bin?'

Eleanor was sitting with her head in her hands, staring into the bowl of cornflakes. She did not move, exactly, but all the slackness left her body as the muscles tensed. 'It got ruined. Wine. Red wine spilled on it.'

'Oh, but Mum, it's your favourite. What about dry-cleaning? Maybe, if I get this tomato sauce off it quick . . .' Rowan reached into the bin and began to ease the dress out but Eleanor sprang from her chair and slammed down the lid.

'No! I don't want it! Leave it!'

Rowan stared down at the corner of green velvet poking from the bin, and she bit her lip. Too late, she realized what she had dragged out into the open. This dress was part of the thing that had happened to Eleanor, and now Eleanor would tell her everything.

'Crushed velvet, you see,' said Eleanor. 'Stains never come out of crushed velvet. And, look, I'm sorry about last night, about shouting at you. I was – upset. That's why I came home early. I – I know you must be wondering why.'

'No. I'm not. You don't need to—'

'It just didn't work out, that's all. I felt really out of place. It was obvious that I wasn't wanted there, so I left. And I was upset about it but I'm fine now, so don't worry about last night. Don't worry. I don't want you to worry.'

Rowan kept her head down, waiting.

'That's it,' said Eleanor.

Relief washed over Rowan as she realized that Eleanor understood the power of names, too. 'OK,' she said, and put her arms around her mother. It was like hugging a block of wood.

After a few seconds Eleanor stepped backwards out of Rowan's arms. 'I'm going to have a bath,' she said, heading for the door.

'All right.' Rowan watched her walk away and saw that her normal, fluid stride had been replaced by a stoop-shouldered shuffle which made her look much older. Rowan suddenly felt very ashamed. I should be helping, she thought, but the relief was still strong in her – stronger than the shame – and Rowan let Eleanor go.

Two essential ingredients of Eleanor's bath routine were loud opera music and a view of the valley.

Rowan had bought her a waterproof cushion one Christmas so that she could lounge against the bath taps in comfort as she gazed out at the high moors through the open bathroom door. Eleanor swore it was an inspired present, the best gift of all time, and she had used it ever since. Until now.

Rowan stared at the locked bathroom door and then at the silent CD player and she longed for something normal to happen. With a sigh, she tapped on the door.

'Mum? Mum, it's twelve. I should be going now, to Alders News . . .'

'Off you go, then,' Eleanor called.

'I – don't have to go to work. I could stay at home . . .'

'What on earth for?' said Eleanor in a bright, brittle voice.

'Nothing . . . Are you OK?'

'Stop worrying about me.'

Rowan leaned against the door for a few seconds, waiting for Eleanor to remind her about her cycle helmet or ask what time she would be back, but Eleanor was silent.

'Bye, then,' she yelled and ran out of the barn, slamming the door behind her. It was the hottest part of a hot day but Rowan put her head down and power-pedalled away from the barn. She rode so fast she forced a breeze out of the windless day and made her tyres sing along the quiet Sunday roads. The grey, shadowy thing was blown away and the helpless feeling went with it and that made her feel so good, she pedalled even harder. The bike leapt forward, a streak of sun-flashing chrome, and Rowan controlled it all, the wind and the road and the racing wheels, all the way into town. She leaned into the last bend and screeched to a stop outside Alders News, panting and sweating and so full of a shining energy that strangers trudging by with dogs and children and fat Sunday papers lifted their heads and smiled at her.

It did not take long for the first shadowy tendrils to come sliding through the door into the shop. I hope she's all right, thought Rowan and lost track of the change she was counting. She stared down at the open till drawer and the man at the counter sighed and held his two ice lollies at arm's length, as though they were about to melt instantly.

'Sorry,' said Rowan, starting again, and getting it wrong, and starting again. 'Sorry.' She did a lot of apologizing over the next few hours, especially after she had sneaked through to the back and dialled her own number and got no answer.

'Remember, pet – a nice, pretty face, yes?' said Mr Tracy, the manager, who had waddled down from the upstairs flat as usual, even though it was supposed to be his afternoon off. 'A nice, pretty, smiling face,' he added, sliding his arm around her waist. 'A smile goes a long way with a customer. Yes, pet?'

'Yes, Mr Tracy,' said Rowan, giving him a clench-toothed grimace and moving out of reach. She did not smile again, not even when a group of local children stopped to perform their Thunderbird puppet routine outside the shop front, which sent Mr Tracy into a fury, as usual. It was a miserable afternoon.

On Monday, Eleanor called in sick, which was almost unheard of. Rowan was standing at the kitchen window, frowning into the bowl of unwashed breakfast dishes when Margaret tapped on the glass.

'Is Eleanor off work? I saw the car still out there,' she said, rushing into the kitchen when Rowan opened the door. 'And she came home early, didn't she? I thought it was the whole weekend, this course?'

'Um, yes,' Rowan floundered. 'She's – not very well—'

'Oh dear. I'll go and see if there's anything I can do.'

'No! No, she's in the bathroom. She wouldn't like anyone . . .'

'Oh. I'm with you.' Margaret shot back into the kitchen and began whisking cereal packets and marmalade jars from the table. 'That just proves what I always say about hotel food. They put all those fancy twirls and frills on to make it look pretty, charge the earth for it, and give you food poisoning! They don't know the first thing about basic hygiene.'

'Yes,' said Rowan gratefully. 'Food poisoning. That's what she's got. And she hates anyone in the room with her when she's being sick. Even us.'

'Of course!' said Margaret, attacking the dishes in the sink. 'Have you called the doctor?'

'She says it's not that bad.'

'Best thing is to let it run its course, then. Now listen, Rowan. Nothing to eat but plenty to drink. No milky drinks, though. And get her some of that stuff that puts the salts back in your body so she doesn't dehy-whatsit. No, don't bother, I think I've got some. I'll send David over with them, if I can get him out of that spider shed. He's as bad as his dad with that allotment.' She put the kettle on and lifted Rowan's chin with a hand still hot and damp from the washing-up water. 'You look tired, lovey. Have you been sitting up with her?'

Rowan looked up at Margaret's long, thin face, and Margaret bent closer in concern. Her glasses slid down her nose and she pushed them up again with her middle finger, just like IQ. Her eyes were hazel too. Rowan suddenly wanted to tell Margaret everything. She wanted Margaret to roll up her sleeves and sort it all out the way she had sorted out the kitchen.

48

'I've been worried,' she said, and stopped. How could she talk about something that had no name?

Margaret's eyes softened. She reached out and stroked Rowan's hair away from her face, the way she still did with IQ. 'Took me right back, that did, you looking all big-eyed and saying you were worried. Do you remember? That time you stood guard against next door's cat all day and half the night after our David showed you that nest of baby birds in our back lane? That's just what you said then, when we finally found you. "I've been worried."'

'And here you are, still trying to do it all on your own! Why didn't you come over, you silly thing?'

Rowan felt her eyes sting with tears and turned away. 'No need to fuss. We're all right. She's not so sick this morning.'

'That's the spirit!' said Margaret, filling up the teapot. 'Now, have this while it's hot. I can't join you – I'm heading for the half-past bus. Then, when you've had your tea, you'll need to clean the bathroom after her. I know it's not a nice job, but you've got to fight those germs. Or I could do it for you when I get back—'

'No. I've been doing it, Margaret. I've been doing it. Disinfectant, the works. And, listen, don't disturb IQ because I've just remembered we've got some of those dehydration powder things,' said Rowan, smiling fiercely as the lies piled up around her.

As soon as Margaret left, Rowan marched out of the spotless kitchen and banged on the bathroom door.

'Mum? That was Margaret. She thinks you've got food poisoning. I let her think it. Is that what you want?' Her voice came out hard and angry. Why was she angry? Eleanor had not forced her to lie. Eleanor had said nothing at all and wasn't that what Rowan

49

wanted? She banged her fist against the door once more.

'Mother? Is that what you want me to say?' She glared at the locked door, feeling shut-out and shielded by it, both at once.

'Yes, if it keeps them out of the way,' said Eleanor, and her tone was desolate. There was a slight pause. 'You know there's nothing to worry about, though, don't you?' she added, in her bright, new TV-mum voice. 'I'm just a bit tired today. I'll go back tomorrow.'

But Eleanor did not go back. She stayed at home all week and careered around the barn like a badly-programmed robot, leaving a trail of half-finished jobs behind her. Whenever the phone or the doorbell rang, she locked herself away in the bathroom and left Rowan to add more lies to the pile.

It was the strangest time. Somehow, without even talking about it, they agreed to ignore the nameless grey shadow which filled the barn. They lived by scuttling around the edges of it, like sea birds on the tide margin. Solitary sea birds, for they learned to stay apart to avoid the stilted chit-chat and heavy silences that had to be stumbled through when they were together.

The food-poisoning story fitted so well that Rowan began to feel it was true. It explained why Eleanor had come home early. It explained why she looked ill and tired and had no appetite. It even explained the long sessions in the bathroom. Rowan wrapped the story around herself and sheltered inside.

Then, on Saturday morning, all the lies were blown away. A letter arrived for Eleanor, from the college. She took it upstairs to read, while Rowan stayed in the kitchen wondering whether scrambled eggs would be too rich for Eleanor's stomach. She had just lifted an egg from the fridge when Eleanor screamed. The egg splatted on the floor and Rowan raced into the main room, then ducked back under the shelter of the gallery to avoid an avalanche of books. She sidestepped and ran out again with her hands covering her head. At the terrace doors, she stopped and turned to look up at the gallery.

Eleanor was clawing armfuls of her books from their piles and flinging them over the railings. Some were so fragile, they disintegrated in mid-flight, filling the air with fluttering white pages and whirling dust. A few exploded like dandelion clocks as they hit the floor, but most of them bounced and slid into untidy heaps that gave off puffs of dust as each new book thudded down on top of them.

Eleanor was still screaming, but now the scream had words in it. 'He can't! It's all lies! He can't do this!' she howled as she moved along the gallery, bending and lifting and throwing her arms wide. She did not stop until every book was gone, then she stepped forward and stared down at the floor of the main room. She looked at the broken spines and the torn pages, and her eyes filled up with tears. The tears spilled over and drew wet, black lines through the dust on her cheeks. Eleanor lifted her head and looked at Rowan, who was standing with her back pressed against the terrace doors and her hands still clasped over her head.

'Jeff Mason tried . . . He – he tried to . . . to . . .' Eleanor came to a halt. Her hands gripped the gallery rail. Her mouth was open but no more words would come out.

Rowan let her arms drop to her sides. She looked up at her mother and named the shadow for her. 'Jeff Mason tried to rape you, didn't he?'

Eleanor nodded. 'And now he's trying to get me sacked.'

'Jeff Mason? I can't believe it,' said Luke.

They were sitting together on Rowan's favourite rock outcrop on the moors above the valley. The sun was still climbing, but already it was hot and too bright to look at. A cooling breeze from the north carried with it the faint chimes of Bickersford's Sunday church bells. Rowan looked down at the barn on the opposite side of the valley. The stone walls glowed softly in the sun and the wall of glass glittered. It all looked so peaceful from the outside, but Eleanor was in there now, going through Jeff Mason's report about her unprofessional conduct during the weekend, and trying to write down what really happened.

'I just can't believe it,' said Luke a second time.

'I know,' said Rowan, wiping her eyes on her sleeve and clasping her hands to stop them from shaking. 'I'm still having trouble taking it in. Especially sitting up here. It's all so quiet and . . . Something as horrible as that seems almost unreal, doesn't it?'

Luke shook his head. 'No. What I mean is, we know Jeff. He's on the Golf Club membership committee with my dad. He comes to our parties . . .'

Rowan turned and stared at Luke. 'What's that got to do with it?'

'He doesn't seem the type. They laugh at him sometimes, my dad and the other committee members. They say he's like the clubhouse labrador – clumsy and slobbery and mad keen to be in on everything. I mean, yeah, everyone knows he goes after anything in a skirt, but it's not serious. Everyone says there's no real harm in him.'

Rowan blinked. 'No harm? He tried to rape my mother!'

'All I'm saying is, perhaps he, you know, misread the signals? Perhaps when she agreed to go away with him for the weekend he thought—'

'Look, she did not agree to go away with him. It

was a working weekend and she was his co-tutor. The whole of the Theatre Group went too!'

'That wouldn't stop old Jeff trying his luck—'

'Old Jeff?' Rowan scrambled to her feet. 'Old Jeff! You're sticking up for him – I can't believe it.'

'Don't start a scene,' said Luke in a calm, low voice, as though he was talking down a nervous horse. 'I'm not sticking up for him. I'm talking things through. That was why you wanted to come up here, wasn't it?'

Rowan put her hands on her hips. 'All right. I'll talk you through a few things, Luke Wetherby. The first thing is, good old Jeff does not go after anything in a skirt. Jeff Mason only flirts with designer skirts. He goes after the skirts that live up on Bickersford Hill and sit around committee tables and carry tennis club membership cards in their designer pockets. He has never, ever been interested in – how did you put it? – trying his luck with my mum.'

'Hang on a minute. First you say he tried to rape her, now you say he doesn't even fancy her. You can't have it both ways—'

'Oh! Oh, you idiot!' Rowan glared down at Luke. She saw a flash of anger in return, then his eyes turned cold and his face became closed and distant. He turned away and stared out over the valley. Rowan knew from their last row that he would say nothing more now, but she had plenty to say.

'What Jeff Mason did to my mum had nothing to do with fancying her. How can you think that? He did it to hurt her. He did it to humiliate her and to make her feel small and ... and ... powerless. He's a nasty man, your good old Jeff, when he's not doing his labrador act up on Bickersford Hill. You don't know him, Luke.'

She looked down at Luke and he stared past her, remote and miserable. 'Can you hear me?' she yelled, loud enough to scatter the sheep. Luke flinched and then seemed to withdraw even further into himself.

Watching him, Rowan suddenly had a clear image of his parents' house, standing detached and remote on Bickersford Hill. She saw the hallway at the hub of the house, with its polished wooden floor and the arrangement of lilies in the fireplace. She heard the steady tock of the grandfather clock, measuring the silence. She pictured the house fanning out from this hallway into cool, pale rooms, with tasteful prints and heavy silk curtains and faded Persian rugs. It was a house that demanded soft voices and restraint. There was no place there for shouting or anger or telling painful truths.

He's like their house, she realized. They've designed their son to match their house. It's not his fault he pulls down the shutters every time anything loud and nasty tries to get in. Still, who am I to talk? I didn't want to know about this either. It took me a week to face up to it and then I was pushed. I'll give him a week, maybe two.

'All right,' she sighed. 'Luke? You won't tell anyone about this, will you? Not even your parents?'

Luke shook his head.

Rowan sat beside him, close, but not touching. 'No, I don't suppose you will, if you can't even talk about it with me. . . When you can talk about it, let me know, because I need some help on this. Can you take me back now, please?'

The look of relief on his face was unmistakable.

Eleanor was still sitting at the kitchen table with the report spread out in front of her when Rowan got back. Rowan could see that parts of every page were heavily underlined in red ink and notes were scrawled across the margins. The toast and coffee she had made for Eleanor stood, untouched, where she had left them.

'Listen to this,' said Eleanor, without even looking up. 'Will you listen to this? The only thing that isn't a lie is this bit at the start, where he says he asked me on the course on the advice of the Head of Faculty, "to cement our professional relationship". That's true all right. He told me he'd been forced into asking me as soon as I got there. And to think I believed he was trying to call a truce.'

'Have you eaten anything yet, Mum? Do you want a cup of tea?'

Eleanor shook her head, impatiently. 'No, no. Look, here where he says I arrived over an hour late for the start of the course – he told me it was seven o'clock, not six! I know he said seven!' She looked up at Rowan for a second, then back to the report. Her hair was wild, her face was still streaked with the dirt and dried tears of the day before and her pink polo-necked top was striped with grime from the armloads of dusty books.

Rowan had tried to get her to eat, or wash, or change her clothes, but Eleanor would do nothing but go through the report again and again, round and round like a cat in a cage, and each time her hurt and anger came pouring out, as strong and fresh as though she was reading it for the first time.

'Look, here! Where he says I arrived at dinner in jeans and a T-shirt, even though I knew the tradition was to dress for dinner on the first night.'

Rowan bit her lip and sat down next to Eleanor. It was like sitting next to a high-voltage power line. She looked at the passage Eleanor was stabbing with her red pen, feeling compelled, once again, to take part in this exhausting, circular performance. She told herself that maybe Eleanor needed to keep picking away at the attack – that to stop her would be bad – but the reality was, she did not know what else to do.

'See that?' said Eleanor. 'Well, he didn't tell me about dressing for dinner! And there, he says he sent me all the details of the course weeks before, but the only thing I got was that scrappy little memo. That's all!'

'I know, Mum.'

'And I threw that away. I wish I hadn't now. He set me up, you know. He set me up.'

'I know.'

'All that rubbish about me not being prepared for teaching – I didn't know I was supposed to be doing something on Elizabethan theatre until five minutes before the session started! I managed, though. I managed to get through all the things he set up to make me look unprofessional, so he could pretend to be the tolerant boss in front of his precious group.'

'Oh, Mum, why did you put up with it? Why didn't you just come home?'

'Because he was expecting me to go to pieces or end up in tears, I know he was. And that made me determined not to. So, I was still there, still smiling, when they got together for a drink on Saturday evening. He was probably thinking I wouldn't make an appearance, but I put on my green dress and brushed out my hair and I made myself to go down there. He was so angry when I walked into the bar, I could see it in his face. It made him so angry, he . . . he . . .'

Eleanor began to cry.

'Don't, Mum. Shhh,' begged Rowan, her own voice thick with tears. Eleanor picked up the pen and began to scribble with short, fierce strokes. She frowned at the pen point and the darkening square of red ink and found her voice again.

'They were talking about the next play they were planning to put on. There were a lot of in-jokes flying around and they were all laughing, especially him. I was sitting there, smiling away and completely shut out. I remember thinking: how am I going to get through another hour of this? That's when I decided to phone you. I thought if I could just hear your voice, I'd feel better. You know?'

Eleanor looked up at Rowan and nearly lost her hard-won control. She zoomed in on the pen again, and scribbled and scribbled. The ball point rasped, the ink darkened and the paper turned thin and shiny.

'I got up and walked out of the bar. They all stopped laughing to watch me leave. They probably started complaining as soon as I'd gone and he probably said something noble and patient like, "Well, if that's how you feel, then I think I ought to go and have a quiet word with Eleanor."

'The pay-phone was in a little coffee bar that was all closed up in the evening. I remember I went in and just sat there in the dark for a few minutes, getting myself together. Then I put on the light and I was halfway across the room to the wall phone when he came in and locked the door behind him.'

The scribbling intensified until the pen broke through the paper and began to score red lines on the table top. Eleanor seemed to be having trouble breathing. She dragged air into her lungs and rushed on. 'I turned round and opened my mouth to say something about wanting to make a private call but I never got the chance. He just threw himself at me. The look on his face – so much hate – I never realized ...'

She jumped up and wrapped her arms around herself, staring up into the far corner of the kitchen ceiling. Her eyes were wide and the tendons stood out on her neck as she fought to find the next breath. She stayed in that position, straining upwards, as though she was trying to climb away from what she had to say next.

'It was very quiet. He didn't say a word and I couldn't. I always thought I'd scream and yell but I'd had all the breath knocked out of me when I hit the floor and then he had his whole weight on top of me and his mouth over mine, so I couldn't—' She stopped for another breath. '—I couldn't find any air. Then he sat up and pulled the skirt of my dress up over my face. He bunched it up, all that heavy velvet, and he held it there with one hand and I still – couldn't – breathe – and I couldn't – see – and he was touching me all over. I was suffocating and my arms were tangled up in the dress—'

Eleanor whooped in another breath. '—and I couldn't throw him off me. I knew then he was going to rape me and, oh God, I knew I couldn't stop him. He was so strong and heavy and – angry. I couldn't stop him. That was the worst thing of all.

'Then the door handle rattled and the door banged in the frame. He went very still. The handle rattled again and a woman's voice shouted, "How am I sup-posed to clean in here? It's locked!" Another woman down the corridor shouted something about getting the pass key from the desk. The cleaner walked away and he got up off me. I remember pulling the dress away from my mouth and taking these great gasps of air and he just stood there watching me, while he straightened his clothes and smoothed his hair. Then he unlocked the door and walked out, back to the bar.'

Eleanor slumped back on to her seat, shaking all over. 'I must've got out of the room and up the back stairs. The next thing I remember is standing by my bed staring down into my overnight bag. Everything was stuffed in together. There was talcum powder and soap slime everywhere. I'd put in my shampoo bottle without the top on and it was dribbling all over my book. That's when I started crying, looking down at the mess in my bag.' Her voice quavered. 'I couldn't get away fast enough. Out the back to the car and then that a-awful d-drive . . .' Eleanor began to cry, remembering.

'Mum. My poor mum,' sobbed Rowan, cupping Eleanor's face in her hands. They leaned together until their foreheads were touching.

'He won, you see,' whispered Eleanor. 'It only took a few minutes and no words at all. All my work at the college, all my commitment, all my confidence. He trashed it in four minutes, then he just got up and walked away. And it doesn't really matter that he stopped before he raped me. He won. He trashed my life.'

PART TWO

PREJUDICE

One

'What's up with Rowan?' asked Theresa. 'Has she said anything to you, Sally?'

'You know what's up. Eleanor's ill.'

'But don't you think that food poisoning story's wearing a bit thin now? Rowan hasn't let us near the barn for three weeks. There's something else, I'm sure of it. Has she said anything to you?'

'Do you seriously think I'd tell you if she had?' grinned Sally.

Theresa pouted. 'Oh, go on! I wouldn't say anything!'

'Sweetie, nothing personal, but telling you a secret is like posting a letter in a revolving door. It just comes shooting straight out again.'

'Ohhh! Go on, tell me. After all, it is my birthday.'

'Happy Birthday.'

'And it's my party.'

'Great party, Tessie.'

Theresa stamped her foot. 'And that's my dad's beer you're guzzling.'

'Where are your parents, anyway?'

'I sent them out for the evening.'

'Do they always do what you say?'

'Sally! Has Rowan told you anything?'

'All right,' sighed Sally. 'No, she hasn't told me anything.'

'Have you asked?'

'Nope. If she wanted me to know, she would've told me. Have *you* asked?'

'Of course I have.'

'Well then, she obviously doesn't want you to know whatever it is, either.'

Theresa gave a frustrated groan and looked across the room to the group surrounding Luke and Rowan. 'Maybe she's upset because they're splitting up.'

'Tut, tut, Tessie. Don't you think you've had enough birthday presents? No, I think there is something wrong with Eleanor. I know she's not been going in to work because Big Edna in our street says their drama meetings have been cancelled. She's getting really ratty about it. Says she's got nowhere to let off steam without her drama sessions. Tom, that's her husband, he's taken to checking her out through the kitchen window before he steps into the house—'

'But does she know what's wrong with Eleanor?'

'Edna says no one's talking at the college.'

'Ohhh! I hate secrets. Somebody must know something,' said Theresa, scanning the room.

'Well, it ain't us, Tessie, so let's just enjoy your party,' said Sally, turning up the music and dancing out into the middle of the floor.

'And don't call me Tessie!' yelled Theresa, following her.

'Oh, yesss. Look at those two move,' said Oliver Green, propping himself up on his elbows to get a better view. 'I wouldn't mind getting stuck in with either of them.'

'No chance,' said Rowan, from the sofa. 'Theresa's in love with – someone else – and Sally doesn't want a boyfriend just yet. She's too busy.'

'Doing what?'

'She has to get her language A levels if she's going to work abroad.'

'Work abroad? Come off it! She's an estate kid. She'll spend the rest of her life in Bickersford.'

Rowan looked down at Oliver, lounging at her feet. 'What did you say, you creep?'

'Give it a rest, Oliver,' drawled Luke.

Oliver rolled his eyes at Rowan. 'We are talking about Sally Rylance here. Her mother's got five kids, and no husband—'

'They can't help it. It was something to do with the immigration laws . . .'

Oliver sneered. 'You don't actually believe that, do you? And what about her sister? Stuck with a baby at seventeen. No, Sally might say she's not interested in boys, but she's probably just the same as her mum and her sister, putting it about everywhere. And you can't tell me Theresa's not hot for it, either. Look at the way she's dressed. All I'm saying is—'

Rowan kicked his elbow out from underneath him. Oliver fell backwards and sprawled on the floor, rubbing his arm. 'Hey!'

'I'll tell you what you're saying, Oliver,' hissed Rowan. 'It's the old "if a girl says no she really means yes" routine. Followed by the "she's showing her legs so she's asking for it" line. All you need to learn now is the classic double standard, "he's one of the lads but she's a slut" and you'll pass your advanced moron test, no problem at all.'

Oliver looked at Luke. 'Can't you control her a bit better than this?'

Rowan stood up, poured her drink all over Oliver and marched out of the room. For a few seconds everyone was still. Then IQ gave a snort of laughter and that started them all off. Luke got to his feet, picked up a pile of paper napkins and handed them to Oliver. Then he went in search of Rowan.

He found her in the kitchen. 'What's the matter with you?' he said, shutting the door. 'One of your witty put-downs would've sorted him out, no bother. You went way over the top.'

'And I suppose you just can't understand why I got so upset?'

Luke turned to the bowl of Bombay mix on the bench and began picking out all the twirly bits.

'It's been three weeks now, Luke. I've been waiting three weeks for you to say something.'

'How is your mum?' muttered Luke, frowning into the bowl.

'Awful. She can't rest. One of our favourite old films was on the other night. We always used to settle down together to watch the old ones with a box of Belgian chocolates and the phone off the hook. She managed ten minutes of it before she was off looking for something to do. All she ever does is clean up. She's even fixed that handle on the kitchen cupboard. The house is so – clean. It's horrible.'

'Oh.' Luke cleared his throat. 'Did she, you know, get that report done?'

Rowan relaxed. It was going to be all right. They were going to talk about it at last. 'Yes, she sent it in to the college. The hearing's tomorrow and we should get the decision pretty soon after that. She's not very hopeful. Jeff Mason got his story in first, you see. She says it looks bad that she didn't speak out until after she saw his report. And he'll have the whole of his Theatre Group speaking up for him too. They might decide she's making it up to explain why she walked out on the Saturday evening, or to get back at him for writing the report.

'I don't know. I just hope they do believe her, but she's probably right about how it looks. They've suspended her on full pay while the investigation's going on, and Jeff Mason's still going into work. It's so unfair, Luke! She didn't say anything for a week because she couldn't. She was – crushed. She still is. I've seen how she's changed.'

'Yeah. Right.' Luke brushed off his hands and straightened up. 'Come on, I'll take you home.'

Rowan stared. 'Is that it?' she said.

'Well, there's no point in us staying at this party when you're not in a party mood. In fact, let's forget about parties and stuff until this business with Eleanor is over. You've been miserable the last four times we've gone out and people are beginning to notice. And look,' he laughed and spread his arms, 'look where we are now! We're not the sort of people who lurk in the kitchen at parties, are we? It's not our style at all. Look, don't worry about it, OK? I can wait until you're back on form.' Luke smiled and patted her arm, but Rowan shook his hand away.

'You actually think you're being kind, don't you?' she said. 'Giving me sick leave until I'm ready to do my bit again. All performances cancelled until further notice. What do you think we are, Luke, some sort of double act? Doesn't it go any deeper?'

Luke's face darkened and he slammed his fist down on the bench. 'Hey! So I like being popular and I like having a good time. So do you. That's what we've been doing all along. If you want to change things all of a sudden, you'd better tell me what the hell you want instead.'

'I want . . . I want you to . . . I'll tell you what I don't want. I don't want a lift home. I'm going.' She turned and opened the kitchen door, too choked to say any more.

Theresa, IQ and Sally were lined up in the hallway. She put her head down and walked past them out of the house.

'Well, go on then, Theresa,' said Sally. 'She's just walked out of your party. Go and get her back.'

'Why me?' said Theresa, edging towards the kitchen.

'Because,' said IQ, 'that's what friends do.'

'Well, you're her friend too.'

'Yeah, but I think she's a bit off men at the minute. Anyway, it wasn't me she was sticking up for back there with Oliver Green.'

Theresa wavered, but the sight of Luke alone in her kitchen was too much for her. 'I tell you what, Sally. You go after Rowan and I'll see if Luke knows what's been upsetting her.' She shot into the kitchen and slammed the door behind her.

'Rowan's at the stop across the road,' called Sally from the front door. 'I'll go and wait with her until the bus comes and then I think I'll head for home. Say goodbye to the birthday girl for me, if she ever comes out of the kitchen.'

She ran off down the path and IQ was left standing alone in the hallway. He sauntered up to the kitchen door, crossed his arms and leaned his shoulder against it, casually, as though he had just stopped for a rest. Then he put his ear to the crack.

Rowan liked buses. She loved the slow, dreamy drift of a journey where the course was already set and the only thing to do was sit and wait. Some people hated surrendering themselves to the bus, even for a short time. Rowan could spot them easily. They always had the exact fare ready and glared at anyone less organized. They sat right at the front and looked at their watches and craned their necks to see the road ahead.

Surrendering was the best part, for Rowan. Her mind would float off and come back with all sorts of surprising thoughts, the way it did in the last few minutes before sleep. She had solved a lot of problems and faced a lot of truths on bus journeys. As Rowan settled back in her seat, she realized that she had missed riding the buses since she started going out with Luke.

Luke! Stupid, thoughtless Luke! She spent the first ten minutes of the journey concocting elaborate plots which all ended with him locked in someone's kitchen as the wildest party of the year raged through the rest of the house. When she grew tired of that, she turned to the window and gazed out. It was a warm evening, still light, and a moon as pale as the thinnest cucumber slice hung in the sky. Outside one house, children played late while their father worked to soften the raw edges of his new garden.

Rowan sat up straight, suddenly realizing where she was. The bus was trundling around the small estate that had been built at the bottom of Bickersford Hill. Jeff Mason had put his name down for one of these houses when they were nothing more than muddy squares marked out with pegs and string. Eleanor had laughed when she heard about it. 'Jeff's bought what he always wanted,' she said. 'A Bickersford Hill address. No house – just the address.'

Rowan looked at the neat row of houses. He's here somewhere, she thought. Maybe even in this road. For the first time since the attack, she contemplated coming face to face with Jeff Mason and the thought made her very afraid. Partly, she was afraid of him and what he had done to Eleanor. When she pictured him now, she saw a man much bigger and stronger than the faintly ridiculous figure she used to see. What frightened her most of all, though, was the sudden rage which filled her at the thought of meeting him. It was all she could do to sit quietly in her seat as the rage coiled and flexed inside her like a snake trapped in a sack.

The houses drifted past and she searched gardens

and shadowy garages, hunting him out. That could be him, mowing the lawn. Her eyes narrowed as she added a patch of wet grass, a slip of the foot. There! Under the blades he went, screaming and bleeding. But, no, that was too noisy. People would come running to help. Instead, she turned to the car on the sloping driveway of the next house, with the man on his back beneath it. The faulty hand brake gave way, the car rolled, and Jeff Mason kicked his life away in silence, with his throat crushed under the wheel.

The bus rolled on, through an estate basking in the evening sun and Rowan stared from the window, making ladders fall and chainsaws twist back on themselves. But she did not spot Jeff Mason and, slowly, the rage settled. She unclenched her hands and smoothed out her crumpled bus ticket. So, it's the Anger Express tonight, is it? she thought, wiping her clammy palms on the seat. All right. That's two dealt with. Anyone else I'm angry with, while I'm here?

Yes, came the reply. Eleanor.

Rowan became very still. No. I'm not angry with Eleanor, she thought. How could I be angry with Eleanor? But all she seemed to see from the window now were mothers and daughters, doing things together. One pair took bags of shopping from the car and Rowan thought of the empty freezer at home. Two more sat on their doorstep, chatting with friends and a third pair lounged together in their front room, watching television. Rowan covered her eyes with her hands.

It wasn't fair! She had worked so hard at her exams and she should be having a glorious time now. The old Eleanor would have turned the summer into a theatrical event. She would have organized days at the beach and shopping trips to the city. She would have filled the barn with friends and music and wonderful cooking smells. Instead, the barn was empty and silent and Rowan had grown to hate the smell of disinfectant and the taste of cold delivery pizza. Yes, she was angry with Eleanor, in the unreasoning, selfish way a child could be angry. She was angry because she had lost her mother and she wanted her back.

'Pathetic!' snapped Rowan, causing the man in front of her to hide his *Gameboy* under his newspaper. She opened her eyes and glared at her reflection in the window. After everything Eleanor's been through all I'm bothered about is having my summer holiday ruined. Right, time to grow up. And I know what I'm going to do first.

She jumped from the bus at the top of the hill, raced into the barn and started yelling as soon as she got through the door. 'Mum, you know you said you can take someone with you to the hearing tomorrow? Well, I'll come with you if you want—'

She stopped at the entrance to the main room and stared stupidly at Margaret.

'It's all right, lovey,' smiled Margaret. 'Your mum's told me.'

'Oh.' Rowan stood in the doorway, too surprised to move.

'I told Margaret because, well—' The two women exchanged glances. 'Because I wanted to ask her to come with me tomorrow. And she said yes. Is that all right?'

Rowan slumped against the doorway, weak with relief.

'Oh dear,' said Eleanor, misunderstanding. 'Thank you so much for offering, sweetheart, but I couldn't take you with me – not to something like that. It wouldn't be fair. Oh, don't cry!'

Eleanor and Margaret both rose from the sofa and hurried towards her. 'It's not that,' whispered Rowan, blinking at them through her tears. 'I'm just . . .' Her throat closed up. She stretched her neck until she was looking up into the high rafters of the barn, but the words would not come out. Then she felt their arms curl around her shoulders, one on each side, and suddenly she was bawling at the top of her voice.

'I'm just s-so glad you've told s-someone else!'

Margaret put her to bed as though she was a baby. So much for being grown up she thought, as she drifted off to sleep, listening to the comforting murmur of voices from below.

Eleanor and Margaret went off together the next morning. Eleanor was pale and quiet but she seemed less locked inside herself, as though talking to Margaret had helped. She even gave Rowan a quick hug before she left the barn.

'Good luck!' called Rowan from the door.

'Oh, she'll be fine. Don't you worry,' said Margaret. 'There'll not be much of him left to pick up after Eleanor's said her piece. Ready?' They walked down the path side by side, and Rowan was struck by how different they were. Margaret, dressed in her vivid floral two piece and court shoes, as tall and thin as a stork, and Eleanor, barely reaching Margaret's shoulder, with her wild hair and her soft, flowing clothes.

In everyday life they had nothing in common, yet Rowan was not surprised that Eleanor had chosen Margaret to go with her to the hearing. Their friendship had begun years ago, during the long waits at the ante-natal clinic. Together, they had endured the discomforts of pregnancy and the horror of screaming babies. Margaret had helped Eleanor through the divorce, and Eleanor had supported Margaret through all the years of trying for another baby that never came. They had what Eleanor described as a crisis friendship, and it went very deep.

Not like me and Luke, thought Rowan, waving them off. One sniff of a crisis and we end up fighting. She closed the door and walked through to the main room. It was the first time she had been alone in the barn since the weekend of the attack and she knew straight away that she had to get out.

She went back into the kitchen and dialled the number of the phone box in Sally's street. There was usually some kid hanging around outside it ready to earn a few pence as a runner, but would they be out this early?

'Yeah?' said a squeaky little voice after four rings.

'Sally Rylance please,' said Rowan.

'Oh, yeah!' squeaked the voice, and Rowan smiled. Sally was known in the street as a good tipper since she got her supermarket job. The receiver clattered against the side of the box and Rowan heard boots pounding away down the pavement. She crossed her fingers and waited.

'This'd better be good,' grumbled Sally, just as Rowan was about to hang up. 'I hate cold toast.'

'It's me. Rowan. I need to talk.'

'OK. Mum's working at the Baths this morning. Fancy a free swim?'

Rowan was long gone when Theresa climbed down from the Bickersford bus and crossed the road to the barn. She tried the doorbell a few times, peered through the kitchen window, then walked to the field fence and began to climb. A cow ambled over and Theresa got down again very quickly.

'Shoo!' she said, and waved her arms. The cow was joined by another. Theresa pouted, then cupped her hands and shouted in the direction of the terrace. 'Rowan! Are you there? Rowan!'

'She's out,' IQ said, at her shoulder. 'Can I help?'

Theresa jumped but recovered quickly. 'Oh, hi. I just wanted to see how she was, after last night. You know. Have a chat. . .'

'All this secrecy's driving you mad, isn't it?' said IQ sympathetically.

'Yes,' sighed Theresa, then she pulled herself up sharp and narrowed her eyes at him. 'I told you, I came to see how she was. So don't get clever with me.' She stalked off.

'I know the big secret,' said IQ. 'I found out last night.'

'What?' said Theresa, hurrying back. 'You found out at my party?'

He nodded, although he had not found out until after midnight, when a grim-faced Margaret had come back from the barn.

'They told you and not me? At my own party?' Theresa was outraged. 'Who was it?'

'Does it matter? It's dreadful news, Theresa. I've been watching out for poor Rowan coming back so I could talk to her about it. That's how I spotted you.'

'Dreadful?'

IQ sucked in his breath and shook his head. 'Come back to the shed and I'll give you some of the juicy bits.'

Theresa shuddered, thinking of the spiders. 'Can't you tell me here?'

'No. She might come back at any minute. Come on.' He crossed the road and disappeared round the back of the terrace without looking back. Theresa hovered, torn between wariness and curiosity. What was going on? IQ never gossiped, especially to her. But perhaps the news was so dreadful he just had to talk about it? The bus that had brought her out to the barn had reached the last stop on its route and was chugging back along the road towards her. She could get on it and be back in Bickersford in ten minutes. Theresa walked towards the bus stop, then threw up her arms and crossed the road instead.

The shed was gloomy after the bright sunshine outside. Shelves and benches were arranged around the walls and a long table stood in the middle of the floor. IQ was down at the other end of the table, pouring water into a bowl.

'Come down here,' he said, without looking up from what he was doing. Theresa stared at the narrow gap between the edges of the table and shelves. Then she looked at the ranks of bowls, fish tanks and glass-fronted boxes she would have to squeeze past. A few were lit with fluorescent tubes but most of them were cellar dark. As she watched, something big and black skittered across the front of one of the tanks. Theresa shut her eyes.

'It's all right,' said IQ. 'They can't get out. Most of them couldn't hurt you anyway.'

'Most of them?'

'One or two are poisonous. But they've just eaten.'

Theresa shuddered. 'You – you seem to have an awful lot of them . . .'

'There's only one in each container. They're solitary, you see. Put two spiders in a box and they'd fight to the death. Come on. Come down here. That's it. Now, hold these for me.'

He heaped a pile of little round sponges into her cupped hands, then he took one back, dipped it into the bowl of water and dropped it into the nearest tank.

'So, um, are they hard to look after?'

'Dead easy,' said IQ, reaching for another sponge.

'A bit of live meat every few days, a damp sponge for water, and they're happy.'

Theresa looked down at her hands. 'You mean these sponges have been sucked by spiders?' she breathed.

He smiled at her and took a few more. 'Does that bother you?'

'No. How – how do they get their live meat?'

'I breed it for them,' grinned IQ reaching under the table and bringing out a large tub. 'See?' He lifted the lid on a wriggling mass of fat, creamy maggots. Theresa could not look away. She stared at their glistening, segmented bodies, with the thin black line running from snout to tail. The line was inside the maggots, under the skin, and it squirmed as they moved. At the centre of each one was a pulsing black blob.

Theresa swallowed and tore her eyes away with a great effort. 'Very nice,' she said. 'So. What's the dreadful news?'

'Tell me what happened with Luke first.'

Theresa gave a guilty start. 'What do you mean?'

'You know. You went into the kitchen with him – to find out what you could about Rowan, remember?'

'Oh, yes. He didn't say anything.'

'Of course he didn't,' snapped IQ. 'You were too busy wrapping yourself around him and telling him Rowan was no good! "Oh, Luke. I would never pour beer over your friends and walk out on you at a party—" '

'You were listening!'

'To every rotten word. I'll tell you the dreadful news now, shall I? Rowan's got this friend, you see. And she really likes her but the friend isn't really a friend at all. She only got friendly when Rowan started going out with Luke Wetherby and now, at the first sign of trouble, she's making her move. But

76

– and here's the really nasty bit – she's still pretending to be friendly with Rowan, see? Because she knows there's something else going on and she can't stand to miss out on a good gossip—'

'Oh, shut up! I don't know why you're so bothered about it. You'll be happy enough if I get Luke away from her.'

IQ leaned forward. His eyes were a hard grey. 'Why would I be happy about something that'll hurt Rowan?'

'Everyone knows you're crazy about her. The only one who can't see it is Rowan, because she would never in a million years dream of going out with a long, thin streak of nothing with bad eyesight!'

They glared at one another for a few seconds, breathing hard.

'I forgot,' said IQ, glancing at Theresa's hands, still cupped around one of the little sponges. 'I promised you some juicy bits.' He picked up the tub and emptied the maggots into her hands.

Theresa continued to stare at IQ with wide eyes, refusing to look down. Cold, cooked macaroni. It was like holding a plateful of cold, cooked macaroni. Except it was moving, squirming into the spaces between her fingers. Slowly, she moved her hands over to the tub and let them fall open. Then she wiped them on IQ's T-shirt, up and down. Only when she was sure all the maggots were gone did she look down at her hands. 'You'll be sorry for that. You and her both,' she said, in a voice trembling with disgust and anger. She turned and walked out of the shed without looking up again.

'Keep away from her, Theresa!' he yelled, as she disappeared into the back lane. He picked the maggots off his chest and put the lid back on the tub. 'Tougher than I thought. She didn't even scream,' he muttered. He peered at his reflection in the front of one of the dark tanks then, taking his glasses off, he looked again, squashing down his nose to make it smaller. With a sigh, he jammed his glasses back on and looked past the glass to the spider lurking in the tank.

'Well, I'm prettier than you are,' he said.

Rowan told Sally everything as they balanced on the ledge at the deep end of the pool with their elbows hooked in the overflow gutter. It was a good place to talk. Only the serious swimmers ventured into the deep end, and they were too busy ploughing through the water to seem like an intrusion.

'She's at the hearing right now,' said Rowan, looking up at the big clock on the wall of the pool. 'I hope she's all right.'

'Eleanor can look after herself,' said Sally, but Rowan shook her head.

'No. She used to believe she could look after herself before the attack, but now – it's like something's been broken. She couldn't stop him, you see. That seems to have been the worst thing for her. She's changed, Sally. All that confidence and that way she had of looking right inside your head – they've gone. She can't concentrate on anything and she hasn't been out of the house since it happened.'

Sally stared at her solemnly for a moment. 'Has she got much of a chance at this hearing?'

'She doesn't think so.'

'Then she's very brave,' said Sally. 'That's one thing he hasn't taken away from her. Christ!' She slammed her hands down on the top of the water and glared up into the roof space. 'What a slimeball.'

When she looked back at Rowan, her face was fierce and her eyes were big with tears. 'Listen, anything I can do, right?' She bit off the last word and clamped her lips together.

Rowan saw the tears and a shout of surprise seemed to run through her whole body. Instantly, her own eyes filled with tears too.

'Right?' Sally repeated.

Rowan nodded, unable to speak. She felt deeply grateful, as though Sally had made her a gift by crying for Eleanor. 'Right,' she said. 'Thanks.'

They looked away then and watched the younger kids, falling off floats and flying out of the end of the chute.

'Bet I can stay under the longest this time,' said Sally after a few minutes.

Rowan grinned, took a breath and ducked underwater. She let herself sink to the bottom and crouched there, staring up at the tangle of disembodied legs trailing down from the surface of the water like pale roots.

'I don't know how you do that!' laughed Sally, when she finally came up for air. 'You must have concrete feet. I can't even reach the bottom, never mind stay there!'

'It's a knack,' panted Rowan. 'I just think heavy. It's not a very useful knack though, is it? They don't give badges for it, like Lifesaving or something. Imagine if they did! Beginners' Sinking. Intermediate Walking on the Bottom.'

'Advanced Drowning.'

They clung to the side, giggling. 'Thanks for letting me talk about Mum,' said Rowan when they had calmed down. 'Luke wouldn't even listen.'

'Oh, well. It was unfair of you to expect him to. The poor lamb.'

'What?'

'Get serious Rowan. In all the time you've been

79

going out with him, has he ever done anything except make sure he has a good time?'

'No. . .'

'There you are then. And to be fair, he's never pretended to offer anything more. If you knew you'd paired up with an amazingly good-looking, amazingly selfish git, why did you suddenly expect him to take something like that on board?'

'You really think he's selfish?'

'Look, you just need to watch him for an hour or so to see that. Always making sure he's got the best seat, the best view, the best whatever. And if he thinks he's not getting enough attention, he sulks. You must have noticed that. You must have realized by now that anyone who goes out with Luke Wetherby has to be prepared to work hard and stay cheerful. He's a full-time job.'

Rowan thought about it. 'You know, you're right. I do seem to spend a lot of my time trying to keep him happy. And these last few weeks, when I've been so worried about Mum, it's all been a bit much.'

'I don't know how you've stuck it, to be honest. He must be really good at the sex bit,' said Sally, floating on her back. 'That's the only explanation.'

'Sally!'

'Still, if that's what you want. On the other hand, if you're looking for a boy who thinks you're better looking than he is, what about IQ?'

'Who?'

'IQ. David Pattinson.'

'Oh, I couldn't go out with IQ.'

'Why not? He's a bit stringy right now, but that's only because his muscles haven't caught up with the rest of him. They won't take long, judging by the way he's eating. He's going to be a real looker, that boy, and it'll last, too. He's got the bone structure. I bet he'll still be tall and rangy when he's as old as, oh, forty. Most men are at the pregnant warthog stage by then.'

'Have you finished? I wasn't talking about his looks, Sally. I meant I couldn't go out with him because we're just friends. We've known each other since we were babies. I even shared his bath for two years while the barn was being converted. Of course, I don't remember anything about it.'

'Well, you might think you're just friends, but he's moved on, as anyone with half an eye can see. He would die for you. Haven't you noticed?'

Rowan shook her head. 'No. You've got it wrong this time, Sally. Come on, let's do a few lengths, then I've got to go. Mum'll be back soon and I want to be there when she gets in.' She bit her lip.

'You never know,' said Sally. 'It might have gone well.'

'At least it'll be over,' sighed Rowan.

Two

The letter arrived three days later.

'They put a lot of thought into that decision, didn't they?' said Eleanor, staring down at the brown envelope on the doormat. 'Let's see, if it was posted yesterday ... I was hardly out of the door when they got that typed up. I told you they'd made up their minds before I went in there.'

'Open it, Mum,' said Rowan. 'Please.' She wanted it over with. She wanted their life to go forward and leave the attack behind.

Eleanor hesitated, then whimpered in the back of her throat and snatched up the envelope. Rowan kept her fingers crossed behind her back for good luck, but it didn't work. As Eleanor scanned the letter, her face became set and pale.

'Has it – gone against you?'

'Oh, yes.' Eleanor's voice trembled. 'Even more than I thought. Listen. "In view of the number of witnesses who support Mr Mason ... blah blah ... no evidence of any animosity on the part of Mr Mason ... blah blah blah ... We conclude in favour of Mr Mason ..." Well, I expected all that. Here's the killer, though. "Both Mr Mason and the commit-tee feel that a written retraction is in order. If you comply with this, then Mr Mason is prepared to be generous—" ' Eleanor stopped suddenly and put her hands to her face.

'A written retraction? He wants you to write down that it never happened?'

'How can he live with himself?' said Eleanor, slumping at the kitchen table. 'What do you think goes through his head when he closes his front door at night? His whole life must be a lie. And his wife – what does she think? Or his son?'

Rowan thought about Paul Mason. He was in her year but not in her form. They had moved through school together and he had never said a word to her, or to anyone else as far as she knew. He was a computer fanatic and spent every spare minute of the school week plugged in to one of their terminals. He did not seem to need a social life.

'Paul's in a world of his own,' she said, dismissing him. 'Mum, if you don't write this retraction, will you lose your job?'

'I don't know. Probably.'

'Oh,' said Rowan. She felt cheated, as though she and Eleanor had hobbled and stumbled their way through a three-legged race only to find that the finish line had been moved. She did not want to run this race any more. She wanted to untie herself from Eleanor and move on to other things.

'Mum? What if, say, you did write something – just enough to satisfy them – and only Jeff Mason and the committee saw it and nobody else. Well, then, we could all forget it and get back to normal—'

'Sweetheart. I can't write it. I can't write that I made it all up. Then my life would be a lie, too.'

'Yes. Sorry. I just – I wanted . . .' Rowan shrugged, at a loss for words.

'I know. But things won't go back to what they were, Rowan, however much we want them to. We've just got to find the best way through all this.' Eleanor looked at Rowan for a moment and her face was bleak. Then she seemed to gather herself up. 'I decided last night, what to do if the hearing went against me.'

Rowan looked down at the table, refusing to ask, but Eleanor said it anyway.

'I'm going to the police.'

Eleanor chose an ivory cotton shirt and purple bottoms from the selection of long-sleeved tops and baggy trousers that had replaced her usual summer clothes. She dressed self-consciously, under her dressing-gown, while Rowan sat on the bed, trying to persuade her not to go. When Eleanor turned her back to put on her bra, Rowan could see that the bruises had faded from her arms. Her skin was winter pale.

'Please don't go, Mum. The hearing was bad enough – you can't put yourself through all that again.'

Eleanor sat at her dressing table and squeezed a palmful of gel out of the tube. She slicked back her hair and began to plait it at the nape of her neck. 'It can't be any worse. I'm sure the police will give me a fairer hearing than Jeff Mason's cronies did.'

'But, Mum,' said Rowan, taking over the plait. 'The whole town's going to know. How will you cope? You couldn't even tell me for a week.'

'I've been thinking about that. I do hate the idea of people knowing, because it makes me feel ashamed. But that's not right! Why should I feel ashamed? I've done nothing wrong. Nothing. He's the one. He attacked me. Why should he get away with it?' She looked up at Rowan in the mirror, then absent-mindedly picked up a lipstick and applied it.

'I don't want you to get hurt any more,' sighed

Rowan, tying off the plait. 'I want you to get over it.'

'That's another thing. It's not just me we have to think about, here. He's going to think he can get away with what he did to me if I don't fight him, and then what's going to happen to the next woman who makes him angry? All those young girls on his A level Literature course – I couldn't live with myself if . . . And I might not even be the first. Have you thought of that?'

Eleanor picked up her favourite perfume, but stopped with the bottle poised over her wrist. She frowned and put it down again, then seemed to notice the lipstick she had put on for the first time. She grabbed a tissue and began to scrub, but came to a sudden halt as the red smeared and spread around her lips. Her eyes darkened, remembering, and her mouth drooped at the corners.

Rowan was back there too, in that steamy bathroom, as she stared at her mother's reflection. Eleanor's hair looked wet, slicked back close to her head, her face was pale and the smeared lipstick made her mouth look sore and swollen. Black as a crow's wing, white as snow, red as blood.

'You see?' whispered Eleanor. 'You see why I have to go to the police? I can't just forget it, sweetheart. It's got inside my head and – tainted everything. I don't want to smell nice or look attractive any more, in case people say I asked for it. I feel ashamed of my own body. Isn't that crazy? He's taken so much away – I have to fight back.'

And Rowan nodded, accepting at last.

They all arrived at once. Eleanor drew up in the car as Margaret and IQ crossed the road from their house, laden down with serving dishes. Rowan, who had been watching for Eleanor from her bedroom window, hurried down to open the door.

'Disgusting!' snapped Margaret, when she heard the result of the hearing. 'Isn't it, David?'

IQ was studying Eleanor under his lashes. 'Yes, Mum,' he said automatically, but Margaret was sailing on, regardless.

'That they can get away with treating you like that, in this day and age,' she stormed, slamming plates down in front of everyone. 'It's that man who looks like a camel who's behind this, I'll bet. I was watching him at the hearing, while you were talking, and I could see he'd already made his mind up. The way he kept huffing and snorting – I nearly offered him a handkerchief.' She whipped the lids from her serving dishes and the steam rose, filling the room with appetizing smells.

'Yes, the camel was very obvious about it, wasn't he?' agreed Eleanor. 'That was the Principal. All he was bothered about was the reputation of the college. Better an incompetent woman than a sex-attack scandal. But I don't think any of them wanted to believe me. Most of them were friends of Mason. They weren't at all like that at the police station.'

Margaret's mouth dropped open. 'You've been to the police?'

'Yes. I've been there all morning. I filed a complaint of attempted rape against Jeff Mason.'

'Well! Good for you!'

'Thanks. It was a tough morning. I had to go through what happened twice and they asked a lot of questions, but you know what was wonderful? They believed me. They really seemed to believe me. Detective Inspector Steven Duns and the Bickersford CID team are going to be investigating my complaint.' She experimented with a smile and held out her plate. 'That casserole smells good enough to eat.'

'So, what happens now?' asked Rowan, unable to keep the sullen note from her voice, even though she was pleased to see Eleanor smiling and eating.

'We have to keep this really quiet for a while, because the team have got a lot to do before they can charge him, and they don't want him to hear anything on the grapevine. That way he won't have a prepared statement ready if they arrest him.'

'If?' said Rowan. 'If! You mean there's some doubt about it?'

Eleanor nodded. 'First, they have to make sure there's enough evidence to back up what I've told them. If they can't find enough evidence, they don't have a case, because the law says it can't be just my word against his. Inspector Duns wants to find the cleaner who tried to get into the coffee bar. They seem to think that's important, the locked door. Why did he lock the door if he was only talking to me? Why didn't he call out to the cleaner or open the door when she tried the handle?'

'There, now, you see?' beamed Margaret. 'Straight to the crucial evidence. Aren't our police wonderful, David?'

'Yes, Mum.'

'And talking about evidence, what about those chappies in boiler suits who crawl around on their hands and knees and pick up fluff?'

'Forensic experts, Mum,' said IQ, suppressing a grin.

'Yes, them. Can't they prove he did it?'

Eleanor looked down at her hands. 'Not now. They could have done, if I'd called the police right away. I wish I had, but all I wanted to do was hide away somewhere.'

'Oh, lovey, of course you did. I'm sorry I asked—'

'No. It's all right. The police say a lot of victims feel like I did. They get loads of complaints where it's

87

too late for forensics.' Suddenly, Eleanor slumped in her chair. 'What have I taken on?' She squeezed her eyes shut and clamped a hand over her mouth.

'Fancy a bit of fresh air, David?' said Margaret, hustling IQ out of the kitchen. 'Rowan . . .?'

'Sorry,' said IQ, when they were safely out on the terrace. 'You go back in if you want. Personally, I could do with a breather. That was heavy stuff in there. How are you doing? You were very quiet.'

'Look who's talking!' said Rowan. 'You just sat there, staring at Mum as though she had two heads or something.'

'I couldn't believe how bad she looks, that's all. She's lost so much weight since I saw her last. So, why were you so quiet?'

Rowan shrugged. 'I wish she hadn't gone to the police. I've had enough. That's really selfish, isn't it?'

'No. Mum says you've been very brave, looking after Eleanor all on your own. You won't be on your own any more though, if Mum's got anything to do with it. She's on a feed Eleanor up campaign – you have been warned. And I'm here too, if you need to talk, or anything . . .' He smiled, then pushed his glasses up to the bridge of his nose and looked away.

'Thanks.'

They sat together on the terrace wall, dangling their legs over the edge. 'Great party trick the other night,' said IQ, 'with Oliver and the drink. He's had that coming to him for quite a while.'

'I wish Luke saw it that way,' said Rowan.

'Ah. Yes. Are you still . . . is he still . . .?'

'My boyfriend? I don't know. I tried to talk to him, about Mum, you see, and he couldn't handle it. Sally says I was expecting too much of him, but what's the point of being a couple, if you can't get serious? Anyway, I think it's up to me to sort things out, since it was me who walked out on him.'

'Do you want to? Sort things out, I mean.'

Rowan frowned out over the valley and IQ became very still beside her. 'I think so. We've been together for nearly nine months now. You don't just throw that away without trying to sort things out first.'

'In that case,' said IQ, taking a deep breath, 'I would get sorting pretty sharpish, if I were you. There's probably a queue forming outside his house already.'

Rowan giggled. 'I'll phone him. Tonight.'

'And that reminds me,' said IQ, casually. 'Have you seen Theresa, since the party?'

'No. I ought to get in touch. I hope I didn't upset her, storming out like that.'

'Oh no, she wasn't upset. She had a very good time after you left.'

'Still, I should—'

'I wouldn't bother with Theresa. She wasn't thinking about her party at all the last time I saw her. She was very busy with something else. In fact,' he narrowed his green eyes and gave a surprisingly wolfish grin, 'she really had her hands full.'

Rowan telephoned Luke that night. She had it all planned. She would be bright and cheerful. She would make a joke or two about the party, then suggest a game of tennis at his club the next day. That should do it. Luke loved playing tennis with her, because she was good enough to make the game flow but not good enough to beat him. As she dialled his number, Rowan smiled, in preparation.

'Luke Wetherby here.'

'Hello, Luke Wetherby. It's your favourite tennis partner.'

There was a pause. 'Hello. Hang on. I'll go upstairs.' He put the receiver down and she heard him call, 'It's for me. I'll take it in my room. Hang up down here, will you?'

His footsteps receded across the wooden floor of the hallway and another pair of feet tapped up to the phone. There was a rustle, then the sound of breathing, but the person on the other end said nothing, so Rowan kept quiet too. With a loud click, Luke was back on the line.

'OK, Mum. You can hang up now.'

'So,' said Rowan, brightly. 'Are you going to let me beat you at tennis tomorrow?'

There was another pause, even longer than the first one, then Luke said, 'Mum. Hang up the phone.'

'Oh, hello Mrs Wetherby,' said Rowan.

'Don't be too long, Luke dear,' said Mrs Wetherby. 'Think of the bill.' Then she hung up without a word to Rowan.

'What is she on about? I'm calling you!' said Rowan, but Luke did not laugh. She ignored the hollow feeling in the pit of her stomach and breezed on.

'We could have a drink in the club afterwards. And I promise not to pour it over anyone.'

'There's – a bit of a problem with tomorrow,' said Luke. 'Jeff Mason was round here for dinner last night and, well, he was making sure everyone knew about the hearing and how he'd won. Anyway, Eleanor came out of it looking pretty bad, the way he told it. He's got my parents believing she made it all up to get back at him for daring to criticize her.'

'But, didn't you say anything?'

'Absolutely not,' said Luke, promptly. 'You told me not to say anything to anyone.'

'But I didn't mean—'

'So,' Luke rushed on. 'They're not too keen on me and you any more. They've confiscated my car keys until, well, coming to my senses was how they put it. . .'

Rowan said nothing. She was remembering what Eleanor had said. 'If they really wanted him to stop seeing you, they'd just threaten to take his car away.'

'Leave it with me,' said Luke. 'It might all blow over soon. If not, I'll try and talk them round.'

'Can't you get the bus for a while?' asked Rowan.

'Hahaha!' laughed Luke, passing it off as a joke. 'Good one, Rowan. I'll get back to you. I promise.'

Luke hung up and Rowan stared at the telephone. He had not even asked how they were coping with the hearing result. 'That's nine months down the drain,' she said, but then drew back from the finality of the words. Give him a chance, she thought. Maybe he'll stand up to his parents. Surely he'll tell them that I mean more to him than his car. Surely?

The investigation took them into a new phase. Eleanor drew strength from the fact that the police believed her, but the waiting was hard. The police were in charge now, and all they had to do was keep quiet. They stayed in the barn, mostly, to avoid awkward meetings with people who did not know their secret.

Time slowed. Sometimes it seemed to Rowan that they were floating behind the glass wall of the barn, suspended like two fish in a tank. Yet, when Big Edna phoned with the good wishes of the drama group and asked, hesitantly, whether chocolate cake was on that weekend, they were both shocked to realize that a month had passed since the assault. Eleanor made vague promises about starting the tradition again soon, then put down the phone and burst into tears. Hearing Big Edna's voice had made her realize how much she was missing work.

91

At last the first call came from the police and it was good news. They had found the cleaner and, not only had she confirmed the locked door and the silence when she tried the handle, she told them she had seen Eleanor running out to the car not long afterwards.

'Oh, that's brilliant!' beamed Rowan.

'There's more,' said Eleanor. 'She also remembers the mess my room was in when she came to clean it the next day. It showed that I must've been really upset when I packed my bag. She told Inspector Duns I'd left a load of stuff behind and, when they went to look in the lost property cupboard, it was all still there, in a plastic bag with the date and the room number on it! They're going to submit that as evidence if the case gets to court.'

'Have they got enough for a case, then?' asked Rowan.

'They seem to think so. The barman who was working on the Saturday evening remembers a lot, too, because we were the only group in the bar that night. He remembers Jeff Mason following me out, then coming back on his own. And, he says Mason was behaving a bit oddly afterwards, turning to look at the door a lot and not really listening when people spoke to him.'

Rowan clapped her hands with delight, and Eleanor smiled. 'So, we're over the first hurdle, sweetheart. The police think they have a case. Now they've got to submit it to the Crown Prosecution Service and their lawyers decide whether the case is strong enough to go to court. They won't let it go ahead unless they think it's got more than a fifty per cent chance of getting a guilty verdict. Detective Inspector Duns says we're not to hold our breath and he'll let us know as soon as he gets the result.'

Three more weeks of the summer holiday drifted

past. Luke did not phone and Theresa always seemed to be out when Rowan called. She went out with Sally, shopping or swimming, and she worked at Alders News, but the barn and the telephone kept pulling her back. The only time she completely forgot about it was when she and IQ cycled up to the moors, left their bikes behind a rock and tramped up to the top of the tor. They sat quiet for a long time, enjoying the high wilderness and the peace. Rowan rested her head against IQ's shoulder and was nearly asleep when he nudged her and pointed to a sunny rock. An adder was basking there, as limp and still as an empty sock. The wind was blowing their way, so the snake's flickering tongue could not detect them. It stayed for twenty minutes, following the sun across the rock then, with a twist of its trowel-shaped head, it disappeared.

Rowan longed to be cold and self-sufficient like the snake. She wished she could lie out on the terrace in the sun and ignore the edgy combination of anxiety and boredom that filled the barn and reminded her of an airport departure lounge. Sometimes, when Eleanor did something completely out of character, like polishing the door handles, Rowan wanted to shout at her to stop. She wanted to clear the air with one of their splendid arguments, but she did not dare. Eleanor looked so fragile now. What if she broke? Rowan found herself snapping at Sally and IQ instead and they, in turn, held back for her sake.

The waiting ended early one morning, the day before the GCSE results were due out. Rowan was still asleep, and dreaming that she had failed them all, when Eleanor shook her awake.

'Good news!' said Eleanor.

'I passed?' mumbled Rowan, struggling up on to her elbows.

Eleanor laughed, and kissed her. 'I'm sure you have,

but that's tomorrow. No, I mean I've just spoken to Inspector Duns. The Crown Prosecution people have told them to go ahead! They've located him and they're going to bring him in now.' Eleanor laughed again, and hugged herself. 'This is the best bit. Do you know where he is? He's playing golf. They're going to arrest him at the club, in front of all his mates from Bickersford Hill!'

Rowan was doubly nervous the next day, when she walked into the entrance hall of the school with IQ. The bus had been full of whispers and stares, so she knew the news must have travelled fast.

The hall was packed and very noisy. The atmosphere was tense. There was a scrum in front of the notice board where the results were pinned, and a more orderly queue at the reception window collecting their slips of computer paper. Everywhere, people stood, looking at their slips with dazed grins or stony faces. A few were crying. Everyone was too busy comparing results to notice Rowan, and she began to relax a little.

Sally waved frantically from the other side of the hall until Rowan spotted her. She held up her slip and grinned, then pointed at them both and put her thumbs up.

'Oh, I think we did OK,' gasped Rowan, clutching IQ by the arm.

'I'd like to see it in black and white, though,' he said, watching from the corner of his eye as Theresa struggled through the crowd towards them, with a vicious look on her face. 'Come on!' He hustled Rowan in front of him away from Theresa, in the direction of the notice board. A strange thing happened, then. The noise and movement carried on around them, but Rowan seemed to move forward in a bubble of space and silence. All the way to the notice board, people stopped talking and looked round, sensing the quiet behind them. Something like shock flitted across their faces and they fell back to let her through. When they closed in again and started to talk, the topic had changed.

'Rowan! Rowan Fletcher,' they said, nudging the ones who had not seen, and soon everyone in the hall knew she was there. Rowan stood at the board and tried to make sense of the closely typed hieroglyphics in front of her. She could feel her cheeks burning and she strained her ears, trying to pick words out of the babble of voices.

'Psst, Moses,' hissed IQ. 'Remind me to take you with me the next time I go to a football match.'

She looked up at him and he made crowd-parting movements with his hands. She let out her breath and smiled.

'There you are,' he said, pointing to the board. She stared at the letters next to her name.

'All of them? I passed all of them!' Rowan flung her arms around IQ's neck and, after a second, he hugged her back.

'What about you?' she said, tilting back her head to look at the board again. 'Oh, brilliant! You got them all too! And look at Sally's language grades – the girl's a genius! Where's Theresa? Oh, dear, she didn't do too well. She's only got—'

Rowan stopped, suddenly aware that she was burbling away in a totally silent hall. She let go of IQ and turned around.

Paul Mason was standing in the doorway.

It was so quiet, everyone could hear the receptionist behind the window telephoning the staffroom for help, even though she was whispering. Paul looked at the crowd as though he was seeing his worse nightmare come true. After years of sitting on the outer edge of every classroom and eating his sandwiches in the humming security of the computer room, he was suddenly the centre of attention. He rose up on to his toes, ready to run, but the need to know his grades was stronger. He ducked his head and scurried to the notice board.

Rowan stepped out of the way and he came to a halt in front of the board. His gaze skidded over her without recognition and he stared at the lists of results with blank eyes. The crowd watched, expectantly.

He can't read it, she thought. He's too nervous. Just like me. Except there's nobody with him to help him out. She cleared her throat, licked her dry lips and pointed to his name on the board.

'H-here you are, look Paul. You've done really well—'

'Don't you dare speak to him!'

Rowan and Paul turned together and stared at Theresa.

'I don't know how you've got the nerve, after what your mother's done,' Theresa snarled, yanking Paul over to stand beside her. 'What a slag!'

Rowan was so shocked, she actually fell back against the wall as though Theresa had pushed her. 'She's not a – a –'

'Of course she is! Look at the way she lives, out there in that cow barn without a husband – inviting half the town in, even though she hasn't cleaned up for years. She walks around without any clothes on – I've seen her. I was there.'

'She'd just had a bath, that's why. And she wouldn't've come out of the bathroom like that if she'd known you were there. And you were only there because I invited you, Theresa. I thought you were my friend!'

'Not any more,' said Theresa, sending a triumphant

glance at IQ. See? said the glance. Told you you'd be sorry.

'Let's get out of here,' said IQ, trying to steer Rowan around Theresa to the door, but Theresa sidestepped, dragging Paul with her.

'Theresa,' said Sally, stepping in front of Rowan. 'You need to move out of the way. Now.' Her voice rang with such authority that Theresa took a step back, then another. Her eyes dropped. Then Oliver Green stepped out of the crowd behind her and put his hands on Paul's shoulders.

It was like striking a match. The atmosphere, already fuelled with so much triumph and disappointment, caught fire. Suddenly, one crowd became two as each person made an instinctive choice and moved to stand behind Paul or Rowan. The few who were left moved quickly to the other end of the hall and clustered there, like a nest of startled owls.

'Well,' sneered Oliver. 'What have we got? Green-law scroungers, lefties and tarts. What a bunch of losers.'

'What would you and your Bickersford Hill lot know about losing, or winning, daddy's boy?' said Sally in a silky soft voice. 'Run away and hide behind your parents, or we might just make you – cry!' She yelled the last word, springing forward and laughing when he flinched.

'Oh, please,' said IQ. 'This is Bickersford, not the Bronx. Why do I have this awful feeling you're all going to start clicking your fingers and dancing any time now?' He laughed, but no one else did. 'You know? Like in that old musical?'

'Shut up, spiderman,' said Oliver.

'Shut up yourself, creep,' called someone from behind Rowan. They all started shouting then, calling names and crowding forward.

'Oh, no!' wailed Rowan. 'There's going to be a fight.'

The clanging brought them all to a halt, with their hands over their ears. Paul Mason had taken the old school bell from its display case and was swinging it back and forth over his head. When he was sure he had their attention, he flung the bell down and stood there, panting. His voice, when he spoke, was soft and rustled in his throat. He used short, chopped sentences, hurrying towards the silence after each full stop.

'I don't want this. You don't care about me. This isn't about me. I want you to stop.' Abruptly, he turned and walked out of the hall.

'That goes for me too!' yelled Rowan, and she ran out after him.

'Paul! Paul, wait! I didn't want—'

'Listen,' interrupted Paul, turning to stare at Rowan with an intensity that stopped her in mid-flow. 'Just listen. I don't want to talk about whether or not he did it, but I think you should know, my father always wins. Always. I know this.' His face twisted and he turned away, struggling to control himself. 'I know. He will fight and fight, on and on, until he wins, because in his mind he is always innocent. Even if he did it, he will have – changed it in his mind. He never admits he is wrong. I'm trying to warn you. It's only fair—' He broke off then, as Sally and IQ came running up.

'All right, Rowan?' said Sally. 'Sorry about that. Oliver Green makes me want to spit. And as for Theresa—'

'What's happening in there now?' interrupted Rowan, not wanting to think about Theresa.

'Don't worry,' said IQ. 'It's not a massacre. Things are a bit cool, that's all. They're all edging around each other, looking sheepish. The teachers are in there now, interrogating, but nobody's talking.'

'They should've been there all along, instead of lurking in the staffroom! That was really nasty, for a minute. It was weird, the way it just flared up. You were right, Paul,' said Rowan, turning to include him. 'They weren't really bothered about us. . .'

But Paul had walked away without any of them noticing. Rowan stared after him, thinking about his warning. My father always wins.

Suddenly, she felt very cold.

Three

The wheels began to turn. There was a knock at the door early the next morning. Rowan opened it, expecting the postman, and found herself face to face with the college Principal. She had never met him before, but she recognized him immediately from Margaret's camel description. A woman stood beside him, clutching her handbag to her chest. The Principal smiled his professional smile for two seconds, then snapped it off again.

'Good morning, my dear. Is your mother in?'

'Yes.'

'Ah, good.' He tried to step inside, but Rowan did not move.

'We would like to speak with her,' he said, in a slow, loud voice. 'If we may.'

'I'll see,' said Rowan, also in a slow, loud voice. Then she shut the door on him.

'We all know who's been on to him,' sighed Eleanor, when Rowan told her.

'You don't have to talk to them.'

'No. I want to hear what he has to say.'

'So good of you to see us,' gushed the Principal, sliding into the kitchen when Eleanor opened the door. 'Shall we talk here, at your little kitchen table? Charming. Charming.'

The woman scurried after him and sat down, still clutching her handbag. She swiped one finger across the table top and looked at it, then craned her neck to inspect the room. Rowan and Eleanor stared.

'Ah, I thought I ought to bring my wife with me. We wouldn't want any more misunderstandings, would we?'

'Pardon?' said Rowan.

'He means he's protecting himself, so that I won't turn round afterwards and say he jumped on me,' said Eleanor, in a hard, angry voice.

'Oh, I say,' he gasped. He looked at his wife for help but she just sucked in her cheeks and rolled her eyes. 'Could we perhaps talk without the gi – without your charming daughter?'

'No. I think I'll keep my charming daughter with me – to avoid any misunderstandings. Now what did you want to see me about?'

'My dear, I've come to ask you to think about what you are doing. Do you really want to ruin the reputation of a good man, a professional man? I appeal to your better nature and ask you to drop the charges.'

'I'd like to go back to work,' said Eleanor, abruptly.

'Ah, yes.' The Principal ran a finger around the inside of his collar. 'The college does feel that, as long as you are pressing these charges, it would be in everyone's interests that you should remain suspended – on full pay of course – to minimize the effects of the case on the working life of the college.'

'And Jeff Mason?'

'Jeff – Mr Mason would, ah, continue to attend the college. He does, after all, have the responsibility of a department – others relying on him – administrative duties . . .'

'That's not fair!' said Rowan. 'You should suspend them both, or keep them both. You're just showing everyone that you support him!'

The Principal ignored her. 'Of course, if you were to drop the charges, you would be reinstated immediately. And,' he leaned across the table and lowered his voice, 'I think we could forget the little matter of the written retraction.'

'And if I don't drop the charges?'

'Then the college would review your position when this – business is over.'

'I see. Let me sum this up. You'd like to sack me now, but you daren't do it until the trial is over, just in case he's found guilty. So I'm to be put on ice, and thrown out if he gets off. However, the best thing all round would be for me to drop the charges. Then he's all right, the reputation of the college is safe, and you can get rid of me quietly at a later date.' Eleanor got up and walked to the door.

'Sorry. Not interested,' she said, opening the door. 'Goodbye.'

There were telephone calls too. Sometimes they gave a name, sometimes not. They all approached the subject in a different way, but the message was always the same. Drop the charges. The next people to show their faces at the door were two women from Jeff Mason's Theatre Group.

'Look,' said the redhead with the Armani scarf, 'we all know Jeff's a bit of a flirt, don't we Wendy?' She looked at the blonde one and they shared a giggle.

'The thing is, there's no real harm in him. A pat here, a squeeze there. Where's the harm? Adds a bit of spice, I'd say!'

'Would you? Do your husbands say that too?' asked Eleanor.

The redhead hurried on. 'Just between us, don't you think you might have misread the signals?'

'No. I know the difference between flirting and

attempted rape. I'd like you to leave now, if that's all you have to say.'

The redhead turned nasty then. 'Oh, we'll say plenty more in court, don't you worry! We were there, remember. We know poor Jeff couldn't have done – that. You're a wicked woman, making up such stories. Think of his wife and son.'

'His wife and son are his business. I'm thinking of myself and my daughter. Goodbye.'

Eleanor slammed the door and leaned against it, shaking with fury.

'Mum, I hate this,' said Rowan. 'All these people coming into our house and telling you what to do. They've got no right to come in here and stare around and look so – superior. Why do you keep seeing them? You don't have to see anyone!'

'Oh, yes I do. I'll see everyone Jeff Mason sends and they can say their bit and I'll say mine. It all gets back to him – I want him to know I mean business.'

Eleanor let the vicar say his bit too, when he came round pretending he wanted to help. She matched him Bible quote for Bible quote and Rowan sat in the corner and glowered until he got up and left without being asked, huffing about good Christian men and fusses over nothing. Rowan looked at the dark circles under Eleanor's eyes and resolved to get rid of the next caller herself.

When someone knocked at the door on Sunday morning, she was waiting. She flung it open, ready to lie and scowl until they went away. Big Edna stood on the doorstep, holding a large chocolate cake and flanked by the whole of Eleanor's drama group.

'I know it won't be a patch on hers,' said Edna, thrusting the cake at Rowan. 'But we wanted to let her know we care. All of us. That's why we all came out together. You should've seen me trying to keep this thing in one piece on the bus. Trust us to get a mad driver!' Big Edna shook with laughter. 'Listen! That's him coming back along the road. He's murdering that engine. Now look, Rowan, are we staying or what? Because we can just turn round and get back on that bus, you know. We've done what we wanted to do. What do you say? Be honest now. Shall we go?'

'What, and leave us to eat this on our own?' said Rowan, pushing wide the door.

It was good to have the barn full of people again. The voices and the movement, the clatter of plates and cups drove out the silence. Rowan even managed to put some music on the CD player. She had tried to do it several times before, but had never quite dared. It would have been like shouting in church. She turned the volume up another notch and gazed around. The terrace doors were open and the room was full of fresh air and sunshine. Eleanor was moving around the group, catching up on all their news and, with every connection she made, she seemed to claim back a piece of herself. Her shoulders relaxed, her back straightened, her hair sprang loose from its band. Her hands stopped clutching at herself and began to curve and dance as she talked. She even found her honking laugh halfway through the visit, when Big Edna offered to have Jeff Mason beaten up.

'No, I mean it. You just say the word,' said Edna, tapping the side of her nose. 'I've got some friends who are, shall we say, good with their hands.'

Eleanor laughed again and hugged Big Edna. 'You're a breath of fresh air,' she said, and Edna beamed. 'I'm so glad to see you all. After the other visitors I've had this week, I was beginning to think the whole town must be against me.'

'No, there's plenty out there who believe you,' said Edna. Then her broad face turned serious for a moment. 'The trouble is, the ones with money and

104

clout are all on his side and they always stick together. Remember when that charity wanted to turn the old church next to the golf course into a rehabilitation centre for drug addicts?'

'What old church?' said Eleanor.

'Exactly. Suddenly it was an unsafe building. Demolition order. Wham! Talk about bringing out the big guns. The new clubhouse is there now. So, watch your back – and pray you've got a straight policeman on the case. Right. That's enough of that. Who's game for another slice of this disgusting cake?'

Maybe we will get back to normal after the trial, thought Rowan as she cycled into work that afternoon. We were nearly there today. Nearly, but not quite. She frowned, remembering how the group had perched on their seats in the orderly, dust-free room, being careful with their crumbs and choosing where to put their cups. That was new, she thought. And, of course, the attack hung over their heads like a bad smell that nobody knew whether to mention. Still, it was good, thought Rowan, and she smiled. Perhaps we will be all right.

Mr Tracy was behind the counter when she walked into Alders News. Automatically, she glanced at her watch. Three minutes until her shift started. Rowan hurried towards the back to collect her overall.

'What are you doing here?' said Mr Tracy.

'It's nearly two,' said Rowan.

'But you're not supposed to be here at all.'

Rowan stopped and looked at him. 'What do you mean, Mr Tracy?'

'Honestly! This should have been sorted. They said they were going to phone you. I suppose muggins here is going to have to sort it all out—'

'Who was supposed to phone me?'

Mr Tracy sighed. 'Mr Alder. When he came in to

105

check the takings, he said he didn't want you working here any more. He's taken Laura on instead.'

Rowan turned and looked at the girl who, having emerged from the back room, was now standing in the doorway, wearing *her* overall.

'And muggins here is losing his afternoon off to train her up—'

'Just a minute, Mr Tracy. Do you mean he's sacked me? Why?' Rowan shook her head and held out her hands. 'Why has he sacked me?'

Mr Tracy looked uncomfortable. 'Well, I suppose he was thinking of you in a way. I'm sure I wouldn't want to be stuck behind a counter in the public eye if I had your – family troubles.'

Suddenly Rowan understood. The Alder family lived up on Bickersford Hill. Mr Alder was on the board of governors at the school, along with Jeff Mason. Big Edna was right, she thought. They always stick together. She clenched her fists and glared at Mr Tracy. 'And what did you say, when he said he didn't want me working here any more?'

A mottled pink flush crept up from Mr Tracy's collar line to his cheeks. 'I – what did I say?'

'Yes. Did you suggest that he was not being exactly fair? Did you talk about what a good worker I was? Did you even ask why?'

'Now, you listen to me, missy. I'm not paid to ask why. I do what Mr Alder says. I'm only the manager of one of his shops and I want to keep my job—'

'So did I!' yelled Rowan, seeing the expedition fund grinding to a halt.

'I shall have to have a word with your mother if you carry on. You're making a spectacle of yourself—'

'No,' said Rowan, marching over to the Slush Puppy machine and mixing up a strawberry one. 'This is how you make a spectacle of yourself.' She upended the cardboard cup over Mr Tracy's head and he gave a strangled scream as a cascade of crimson ice crystals slid down the front of his shirt.

'Oops. Sorry,' said Rowan. 'There's another mess for muggins to clear up.'

Laura gave a startled giggle then stepped back as Rowan turned to her. 'Good luck,' said Rowan. 'And watch him. He's a bit of a groper.'

'Good riddance!' Mr Tracy shouted, as she walked out of the shop. 'I always knew you had a wild streak. Just like your tramp of a mother!'

Rowan grabbed her bike and pushed it along the pavement, too shaken to ride. A car horn sounded twice over the road. She looked round and was swept by a thrill of surprise and joy. Luke was sitting there, smiling and waving her over. He had done it! He had stood up to his parents! Rowan had never been so glad to see him. She laughed and waved back, swearing never to underestimate him again.

'Hello!' she called and he turned to look, which made her realize that he had been waving at someone else all along. His smile collapsed. He turned away from her and stared ahead through the windscreen. Rowan looked over her shoulder and saw Theresa coming out of the video hire shop that she and Luke always used.

'My lift, I think,' said Theresa, brushing past her and running to the car.

Rowan did not remember getting home. She must have cycled hard because she could hardly find the breath to shout when she rushed into the barn and confronted Eleanor.

'Why did you have to go to the police? Why couldn't you just write the stupid retraction and forget about it? It's my life too, you know! My life's falling apart and you couldn't care less! I've lost my job and my boyfriend because of you! And school starts tomorrow – I've got to go in and face them all, while you sit at home! I hate you for this! I really hate you!'

She flung herself onto the sofa and sobbed into the cushions. Eleanor tried to hold her and she knocked her arm away, but Eleanor kept trying until finally Rowan let her climb onto the sofa and cuddle into her back. The crying grew until it was so full of power and fury, it frightened her. She was out of control. It was as though she was in a dark box and the box was rattling down a steep track and she could not find the brake. She felt her centre, the part that was Rowan, being shaken apart in that rattling box. She wailed into the darkness as it picked up speed. What if the track ran out? What if the box shot over the edge of a cliff? She might never find herself again.

But Eleanor's arms were around her waist, anchoring her, and Eleanor's mouth was next to her ear, whispering her name. Rowan held on to that and, gradually, she began to slow down and notice ordinary pains. The material of the cushion was rough against her face. Her thigh muscles ached from the ride home. The buttons on her T-shirt were sticking into her neck. Rowan sniffed and opened her eyes. The buttons were really digging in now, so she turned over to face Eleanor. She felt as limp and salty as a strand of seaweed.

'There,' said Eleanor, kissing her sticky face and clearing the hair from her eyes. 'That's better. You haven't really cried since this started, you know. Not properly.'

They lay quiet, gazing into one another's eyes, and Rowan saw that Eleanor had been crying too.

'Mum, I'm sorry for saying I hated you—'

'Shhh. I know. Everyone says things they don't mean when they're angry. Especially when they've

108

held it in for so long. You've been so good and quiet about it all, while I've been stomping around, throwing books everywhere – it had to come out sometime. Now, what happened this afternoon?'

Eleanor listened to Rowan's story and her face grew angry. 'That is awful. Those Wetherbys – I could. . . And the Alders! What are they doing, getting at me through you? Despicable!'

'Mum, I'd better tell you now, in case he phones up and complains,' said Rowan. 'I poured a strawberry Slush Puppy over Mr Tracy's head.'

'Good for you!'

'I shouldn't have done it, really – he's not the big villain, is he? I was just angry at the whole thing. Why is all this happening to us? One minute, we've got a pretty good life going – the next minute. . . It's so unfair! Jeff Mason did something bad and we're being punished.'

'I know. I know, sweetheart,' Eleanor hesitated. 'You don't – you don't really think I should've written the retraction, do you?'

Rowan sighed. 'Oh, no, I suppose not. You did the right thing, Mum, going to the police.'

Eleanor shook her head. 'No. It was the only thing to do, but it's not right. Everything I do is going to be wrong and hurtful, because it's all growing out of the wrong thing that Jeff Mason did to me. It's like a chain reaction. Do you see what I mean?'

'I – think so. . .'

'It's like – do you remember the Oxfam charity thing you all did at school last year? That toy company supplied you with dominoes and you made a huge pattern with them on the sports hall floor.'

'That was a back-breaking job. It took us a week!'

'All those dominoes, lined up and ready to fall. The person with the winning raffle number had to knock over the first domino, remember?'

109

'Yeah, and we were really nervous because the gallery was packed and they were standing at the windows looking in and none of us really knew whether it was going to work. But it did.'

They were both silent for a moment, remembering how the falling dominoes had spread and branched from the centre, swirling and curving across the floor, faster and faster, until the clattering was so loud, it drowned out the cheers of the crowd.

'That's what it feels like,' said Eleanor. 'It's as though when Jeff Mason attacked me, that was only the first domino falling. Everything's spreading out from that single domino, into my life and your life and Margaret's life and the drama group. . . . Clatter, clatter, clatter. It's knocking down my past and my future and there's not a thing I can do about it because, once it's started, there's no alternative but to go on with it. The frightening thing is, I don't know when it's going to stop. How big is the pattern? How far is it going to spread, this domino effect?'

'Domino effect. That's a good name for it,' murmured Rowan, and fell asleep, with her nose pressed into Eleanor's neck. Eleanor put her arms around Rowan and stared up into the roof space for a long time until, finally, her eyes closed too.

The ringing of the telephone brought them both awake. Rowan clutched at Eleanor, unsure of where she was. Her heart banged against her ribs.

'Oh, dear,' groaned Eleanor, sitting up and peering at her watch. 'We've slept the day away. And my leg's gone numb.'

'I'm cold,' grumbled Rowan, clambering from the sofa. The sun was low in the sky and the breeze from the open terrace doors was chilly. The telephone was still ringing.

'I suppose I'd better get that,' said Eleanor, hobbling towards the kitchen. 'Even though the last thing

110

I need right now is someone else telling me to drop the charges.'

'It's probably Mr Tracy phoning to complain,' said Rowan, smiling, despite herself, at the memory of his face covered in red mush.

'Come on then. You can listen.'

They hurried into the kitchen. Eleanor picked up the receiver and they leaned their heads together, cradling it between them.

'Hello. Eleanor Fletcher speaking,' cooed Eleanor, waggling her eyebrows at Rowan.

Breathing.

Eleanor's eyebrows came together in a frown. 'Mr Tracy?'

It was heavy, open-mouthed breathing. Loud. As though the person at the other end had his hands cupped around the mouthpiece.

'Who is this?' said Eleanor, her voice rising.

Words came out of the breathing, then. Slow, measured words, one on each breath.

'I am coming to kill you.'

Rowan watched Eleanor's eyes widen, six inches from hers. She stared into the dark pupils and saw her frightened face reflected there.

'Women like you deserve to die. I am very close. Much closer than you think. I can see you—'

Eleanor slammed down the receiver and ran to the window. She stared across the road to the telephone kiosk at the end of the terrace. 'Empty,' she said, running to the back door.

'Mum!' screamed Rowan as Eleanor wrenched open the door and ran outside. 'Come back!' She stood with her hands pressed to her mouth as Eleanor skidded to a stop on the pavement and did a slow turn, scanning the road and the houses opposite. Then she turned and looked up at the barn. Finally, she bent and picked up Rowan's bike, which was still

111

lying on the grass in front of the barn, and wheeled it into the kitchen.

'Are you crazy? Why did you go out there?'

'Because if I hadn't,' said Eleanor, locking and bolting the door, 'I might have started to believe him.' She slid the chain across. 'There. All safe. And the windows are shut, I had a look while I was out there. Now, listen to me, sweetheart. That was a horrible thing to hear. I know it scared you, but the thing is, if someone really wanted to kill me, he wouldn't ring up and tell me first, OK? That was just a phone creep – nothing more.'

Rowan made a lunge for Eleanor and held her close. 'I was so frightened,' she whispered. 'What if he phones again? What do we do?'

'I'm going to get in touch with the police now. They'll tell us the best way to deal with it. Why don't you put the kettle on? I think we need a hot drink. And put on the light, it's starting to get dark earlier now.'

'How come you're being so cool about this?' asked Rowan, flicking down the light switch.

'Because I refuse to let a little pervert like that frighten me,' said Eleanor. Then she gave a shaky laugh and added, 'But I have to admit I put on a bit of an act out there. Your bike's only in here because I was too scared to wheel it round to the garage.' She went to the phone and dialled the CID number. 'Teapot's still in the main room,' she said, seeing Rowan searching the kitchen.

Rowan set up the rest of the tea things, listening to Eleanor talk to Inspector Duns. It was comforting to move around the kitchen, following a routine, and she began to calm down. Strange, how we still do all the boring stuff, even in the middle of something like this, she thought, hunting out Eleanor's favourite bone china mug with the bluebells on it.

The movies have got it all wrong, she decided, as she went to get the teapot.

A draught of cooler air blew past Rowan as she opened the kitchen door, and she froze in the doorway, staring into the shadows of the main room. Eleanor felt the breeze too, and looked up, stopping in mid-sentence. For a few seconds, they were both absolutely still. The only noise was the questioning squawk coming from the receiver. When Eleanor spoke again, her voice was shaking.

'Inspector, our terrace doors are wide open.'

The phone squawked again.

'Right,' said Eleanor. She hung up, still staring into the main room. 'Come on, Rowan. We're going to Margaret's house.'

Rowan could hear Eleanor unbolting the door and fumbling with the lock, but she could not turn her back on the main room. She took one step backwards, then another. She was concentrating so much on the moving shadows in front of her, she walked into the bike. It fell to the floor with a resounding crash and Rowan screamed. Then Eleanor grabbed her by the wrist and dragged her out of the barn.

It was empty, of course. By the time the police arrived, IQ and his father had checked the whole barn, and they were back in the kitchen, having their interrupted cup of tea.

'The chances are, he's just a crank who picked up on all the gossip,' said Inspector Duns.

'I know! I knew that and still I let it get to me. I should've remembered we'd left the terrace doors open.' Eleanor was near to tears.

'Well, no harm done.'

'But he did harm me! I was frightened to stay in my own house. My own house!' She sniffed and

113

wiped her eyes. 'He won. Do you know, I think that's getting to me more than the phone call? Well, I won't let him beat me again.'

'Good.' Inspector Duns drained his cup. 'Right. To business. He's going to phone again, almost certainly. The best thing to do is leave him talking and go and read a book or something. That way, you don't have to listen and he won't get what he wants, which is a reaction.

'As we said, he's probably nothing to bother about, but it wouldn't harm to be a bit careful about security. And I'm going to put you on the patrol car route for a while. Don't worry, they won't disturb you. They'll just keep an eye on things.

'First thing tomorrow, you need to arrange for a change of number. It'll take them a few days, but once that's done, he's finished. It'll probably stop those other calls I imagine you've been getting too.'

Rowan shot him a surprised look. 'How do you know about those?'

'I've had one or two myself. People phoning, just for a chat you understand, and mentioning their friend the commissioner and wondering whether it might damage my career, taking on a case that's sure to lose – you know the sort of thing. Very delicate.' He smiled. 'I never did like being told what to do. Right, one more thing before we go. Jeff Mason is due to appear at the magistrate's court tomorrow. Just a formality. They read out the charge and ask him how he pleads. He'll say not guilty and the case will be referred to the Crown Court. Pretty soon after that, we should get our trial dates.'

'When do you think that'll be?'

Inspector Duns looked uncomfortable for the first time. 'Not until next year, I'm afraid.'

'Next year!'

114

'Before the spring, if we're lucky – we might get a cancellation.'

Rowan and Eleanor shared a horrified look. How were they going to get through six more months of this?

The phone rang again at two o'clock that morning. Rowan had not slept. She lay, listening to the shrill double tone echo through the barn. Why did telephones always sound louder at night? She counted twenty rings before Eleanor got up and padded down to the kitchen to take the phone off the hook. When Eleanor came back, Rowan scurried into her room.

'I can't sleep.'

'Me neither,' said Eleanor, pulling back the duvet for Rowan to climb in next to her.

'It's the first day of my Sixth Form career tomorrow, and I'm going to look like a panda bear,' sighed Rowan, snuggling down into Eleanor's big bed.

'The domino effect strikes again,' whispered Eleanor, stroking her forehead.

Rowan drifted off, lulled by the stroking, and dreamed that she was edging her way through a forest of towering dominoes, all lined up and ready to fall.

PART THREE

THE TRIAL

One

Scrape, scrape, scrape.

Rowan opened one eye and listened. If Eleanor was clearing ice from the car windscreen, it must be very cold outside. Too cold to cycle to school. She pulled the duvet higher and started making plans. Theresa always insisted on being driven to school in bad weather. She could get a lift with Eleanor as far as the college, then nip over the road to Theresa's house and—

Rowan groaned. No, that was her old life. They were living a new life now; a cut-off, makeshift existence which made Rowan feel like a – a refugee. That was it. She and Eleanor had become refugees without even leaving the barn and Rowan could not stop longing for the life they had been forced to give up. She slid her feet out of bed and sat up, then remembered it was Saturday and curled back under the duvet with a sigh of relief.

School was all right but Rowan did not enjoy it like she used to. The madness of results day had never been repeated. Paul Mason proved to be a poor champion, locking himself away in the computer block and refusing to set foot in the Sixth Form Common Room. Even Theresa had stopped her constant insults, since Luke had dragged her off to a quiet corner after one particularly nasty attack.

'He's not doing it for you,' said Sally, when Rowan pointed out what was happening. 'Theresa was embarrassing him, that's all. You know how he hates to be embarrassed.'

Whatever the reason, Rowan was grateful for his intervention. Without Theresa's sneers and digs, school was bearable, but it was not how she had imagined life in the Sixth Form. The split which had developed so dramatically on results day had never quite healed. The Common Room tended to be divided into two main camps and, even though the boundaries were becoming more blurred every day, there were still some people who refused to talk to her.

At home, there were new rules to remember. The death threats had stopped when their number was changed, but Rowan never gave the new number when she picked up the phone, just in case. They kept the windows and doors locked all the time and Rowan had grown used to waking every night as the patrol car slowed outside the barn and a flashlight flickered across her bedroom window. They bought their newspapers from the petrol station now, instead of Alders News, and they stayed away from the Bickersford Delicatessen since the day the owner had refused to serve Eleanor.

Rowan grimaced, remembering how the woman had glared at them when they reached the counter. 'Hello,' Eleanor had said, trying to carry on as normal. 'Can we have our usual—'

'You are not welcome in my shop,' the owner had snapped, and she had left them standing there while she served the next person in the queue.

Scrape, scrape, scrape.

Rowan frowned. What was that noise? She listened

120

more closely and heard whispers; urgent, hissing whispers. There was more than one person out there.

Rowan jumped out of bed and ran to the window. There was a light covering of frost outside, just enough to whiten the tips of the grass blades but not enough to hide the words that had been scrawled across the pavement in red paint. Margaret and IQ were down there, wrapped up against the cold. Margaret was crouched over one of the words with a bucket of steaming water and a scrubbing brush, and IQ was next to her with a paint scraper in his hand. They were trying to clean the paint from the paving stones. The words were upside down to Rowan, but still the large, bright letters were easy to read.

CHEAP SEX HERE
THEY WILL DO IT WITH ANYONE
FOLLOW THE ARROWS TO SEX

Rowan stared at the line of crudely drawn red arrows marching up the path to her front door, then she grabbed her dressing-gown and ran downstairs.

'Oh lovey, I'm sorry. It won't come off,' said Margaret, when Rowan burst out of the front door into the street. Rowan frowned down at the arrow beneath her feet. The paint looked so bright and shiny, she thought it must still be wet, but when she bent to touch it, it was hard and icy cold.

'Did you see who did it?' she asked, shivering as the cold bit through the thin soles of her slippers.

'No. It was already done when Dad went out to work this morning,' said IQ, kicking at the paint with a grim look on his face.

'Don't stand out here and freeze, lovey,' said Margaret, her own nose purple with cold. 'David's going to paint it out, for now, while we figure out

121

how to get rid of it. You go back in and try to keep your mum away from the windows.'

'Too late,' said IQ.

Rowan turned to look up at the front of the barn. Her gaze halted above the door for an instant, caught by the words staining the old stonework.

HOUSE OF WHORES

She blinked once and raised her eyes higher. Eleanor stood, framed in the bedroom window, with the red words on the wall just below her like a caption. Her dark hair fell in untidy curls and her face was white with shock. Red as blood, black as a crow's wing, white as snow, thought Rowan. She shook her head to chase the words away and sat down hard on the pavement, suddenly dizzy.

That was how the bus full of workers and early shoppers found them, as it trundled past on the way into Bickersford. The passengers looked out at the scrawls of red paint, the woman at the window and the girl sitting on the frosty ground in her dressing-gown, and their sleepy expressions disappeared. IQ moved in front of Rowan, protectively, but not before she saw the row of pointing fingers and open mouths. She rested her head on her knees and wondered how things could possibly get any worse.

'Are you going to tell the police?' asked Margaret, refilling the teapot.

'No,' sighed Eleanor. 'There's no point. It'll be just like the death threats – they won't be able to find out who did it.'

Thinking about the police made Rowan remember how she had woken in the night when the patrol car stopped outside the barn. The big engine had idled for a few minutes before purring off down the hill.

'It must've been done after two in the morning,' she said. 'That's when the patrol car went past. They would have been out checking the barn if the paint was already there.'

'It needed at least two of the little blighters, I reckon. One to lift the other high enough,' said Margaret, looking up at the stained glass fanlight above the door. IQ was out there, standing at the top of Eleanor's stepladder, painting out the words. 'Kids probably, do you think? Although they must've been old enough to drive, to get out here at that time of night—'

'It doesn't matter who it was,' said Eleanor. 'What matters is that they planned this. They had to buy the paint and organize the trip out here – they wanted to do this enough to get out of their beds in the middle of a freezing night. . .' Eleanor shuddered and curled her hands round her cup, staring down into the tea.

IQ broke the silence when he stuck his head round the door. 'All done. I've not used much because it's all got to be cleaned off again, but you can't read anything out there now.'

'Ah, yes. Cleaning,' said Margaret, leaping up and grabbing the *Yellow Pages*. 'What do you think? Sand blasters? Stone masons? Or shall we start with the Council . . .?'

Rowan and IQ left them to it and headed across the road to his shed.

'It's got to be Theresa,' said IQ, closing the shed door and switching on the heater. 'Not that we can prove anything.'

'Why? Why does she hate me so much?'

IQ rubbed his jaw and frowned at the floor, thinking about it. 'Partly resentment for all the time you had Luke and she didn't. And I think she's scared, too, in case he might want you back. She's trying to make sure that doesn't happen.'

'You know, I feel really stupid. How could I think she liked me all those months? You've never trusted her, have you?'

IQ shook his head.

'How could you tell? How did you know, when I didn't?'

'Well, for a start, she changes her accent depending on who she's talking to. I've never liked that. And – I don't know, Rowan. I'm just not as trusting as you are.'

'I can't believe she actually stood outside my house and painted those things about me—'

'Oh, no. I'm sure she didn't come out here herself. That's not Theresa's style. She talked someone else into doing the dirty work. Oliver Green and his mates, at a guess.'

'But not Luke. Luke wouldn't do that. He can't face up to things, but he's not vicious.'

IQ moved over to the table and shuffled his sheets of paper, which were covered with meticulous line drawings of spiders. 'Do you still miss him?' he asked, keeping his head down.

Rowan thought of various answers to that one and decided to be honest. 'No. If you want the truth, I got over him very quickly. Too quickly, really, for anything much to have been there in the first place.' She shrugged, then crouched in front of the big tarantula tank and peered at the dark burrow in the corner. 'How's Tessie doing?'

'She's getting old,' said IQ, rolling up the sleeves of his jumper and opening the tank to put in fresh water. The hairs of his forearms gleamed golden under the fluorescent tube. The muscles moved under his skin. 'She doesn't come out of her burrow much now.

You might see her if we keep still,' he said, crouching beside Rowan. He smelled of clean hair and frost and paint.

'Thanks for this morning,' said Rowan. 'I always seem to be thanking you these days, you and your mum, and Sally. You've all been great, IQ.'

He turned his face towards her. 'Will you do me a favour?'

'What?'

'Stop calling me IQ?'

'All right. David,' said Rowan, and she stared at him, astonished. It was as though saying his real name had made the final connection on a circuit board inside her head. Instantly the power flowed and the board lit up in colours of green and gold.

'David,' she said, again, and he smiled. His eyes looked almost black, with a rim of the softest green.

They leaned towards each other until their lips touched, but it was difficult to hold a kiss as they balanced on their haunches, so Rowan stood up and David followed her.

'If you knew how long I've been waiting for you to do that,' he breathed.

Rowan cupped his head in her hands, pulling his face down to hers. It was not at all like kissing Luke. Luke accepted kisses like a king accepting homage. David shared the kiss with a trembling intensity that excited her. Afterwards, he held her close, so that her head rested perfectly in the hollow beneath his collarbone. She listened to the hard, fast beating of his heart and he pushed his nose into her hair, breathing deeply.

'I've always loved the smell of your shampoo,' he murmured, resting his chin on the top of her head.

Rowan smiled as she traced the curve of his spine with her fingers. Sally was right after all, she thought.

A few minutes later, the tarantula heaved her fat,

furry body out of the burrow and picked her way over to the fresh water. She drank her fill, turned and squeezed back into the hole, completely unobserved.

Rowan found Sally in the detergents aisle, stacking the shelves with boxes of soap powder. Her eyes were red and puffy and she kept sneezing.

'Allergic to the stupid stuff,' she sniffed when she saw Rowan. 'Makes me itch too.' She scratched at her hands, which were coated in a fine dusting of white powder.

'You look tired,' said Rowan.

'Becky's Sam cried all night with his teeth,' said Sally. 'I'm working till eight tonight and I've got a French essay to do for Monday.' She crossed her eyes and pretended to pass out. 'I tell you, after last night, I don't think I'll ever let a man near me, never mind waiting till I've got my A levels. Babies are so loud!'

Rowan thought about the sleeping arrangements at Sally's house. Sally shared a bedroom with Becky and her little sister Avril. The twins, James and Eddie, had the second bedroom and Sam's cot was squashed into the box room, at the bottom of Sally's mother's bed.

'Isn't the baby sleeping in with your mum any more?'

'Yeah, but the walls aren't very thick, you know. Besides, I couldn't let Mum and Becky do it all.'

'Come and sleep over,' said Rowan, impulsively. Then a look of uncertainty passed across her face. She had not had anyone to stay since July. What would Eleanor think?

Sally watched her. 'Are you sure about that?'

'Yes, I'm sure.'

'I heard about the paint job. Chloë at the cheese

126

counter was on the early bus this morning. How's your mum?'

'She's pretty bad just now. We're supposed to be doing the weekly shop but she's rushing round this place so fast, I keep having to go back for stuff we've missed. She hardly goes out at all now, you know. Just stays in and cleans up.'

'Big Edna was asking after her.'

'That's something else. I've been trying to get her to start the cake thing again, but she always says maybe next month. It would do her good to have the drama lot round again. She really lit up when they did their surprise visit.'

'Why don't you just do it?'

Rowan shrugged, at a loss to explain how the quiet misery of the barn stifled ideas like that before they were properly born.

'Has she had no visitors at all?' asked Sally.

'Oh, yes,' said Rowan, brightening. 'I forgot to tell you. Remember Mum's drama group won the prize at the festival this year for the best improvised piece? Well, one of the judges runs that drama school in the city—'

'Yeah, I remember. She offered your mum a job, didn't she?'

'That's right. And she just turned up on the doorstep a couple of weeks ago. She hadn't been able to get through on the phone, because she had our old number. She'd heard about the attack and she wanted Mum to know the job was still on offer. When Mum said didn't she want to wait for the verdict, she said no, she'd worked with Jeff Mason in the past and she knew what he was like!'

'Nice one,' smiled Sally. She stacked a few more boxes, then kicked the trolley she was unloading. 'I'm so bored! Tell me something stunning before this job sends me off my head.'

'Well, you were right. David really likes me.'

'Ooh, David now, is it? Told you he would die for you.'

'And the big surprise is, we're going out together, as of this morning.'

'That's no surprise. Your body knew you liked him long before your head caught on. It's been so obvious these last few weeks. Always touching his sleeve when you're talking to him, sitting closer than you ought to.'

Rowan felt herself blushing. 'Do you think he noticed?'

Sally laughed. 'I think you were the last to know, kiddo. I'd like to stay tonight,' she added, deciding. 'I could do with a night off from everything. I'll come straight from work, OK?' She glanced up, then grabbed a box of soap powder and shoved it into Rowan's hands.

'I think you'll find our own brand is very good value,' she said smoothly.

'What?'

'The cinnamon is two aisles back next to the flour, the muffins are on the bakery and the hot chocolate is over there.'

'Thank you,' said Rowan, catching on. 'I'll go and get those now.' She turned and walked past the advancing supervisor, the very image of a busy shopper.

'That was fine, wasn't it, Mum?' said Rowan, when they were driving out of the supermarket car park, but Eleanor did not answer. Her hands were gripping the steering wheel and her mouth was set in a tense line. She kept looking into the rear view mirror.

'Mum!' shrieked Rowan, as they overshot a junction. Eleanor slammed on the brakes and a car scraped past their front bumper with its horn blaring.

'Sorry,' muttered Eleanor, flicking nervous glances at the mirror while she restarted the engine.

'What is it?'

'Don't look round, but I think that man behind is following us.'

Rowan peered at the dirty brown car in the mirror. All she could see through the smeary windscreen was a dark shape.

'He was parked across our road at the end of the terrace this morning. He followed us down here and now he's following us back.'

Rowan swallowed. 'OK. I'll watch him and you watch the road. I'll tell you if he turns off.'

The man in the brown car did follow them all the way home, but when they stopped in front of the barn, he drove on by and disappeared over the brow of the hill.

'False alarm,' sighed Rowan, but Eleanor stood on the pavement, staring after the car for several minutes, leaving Rowan to carry in the shopping all on her own. In and out she went, trying not to look above the door at the white oblong of paint with the red showing through like blood through a bandage.

'So why did your mum spend half the night at the kitchen window?' asked Sally, from the truckle bed. 'Does she think the paint sprayers are going to do an encore?'

Rowan rolled to the edge of her bed and looked down at Sally. 'No. She thinks there's a man parking his car at the end of the road and then following us when we go out.'

'Oh. Does she think he did the paint job too?'

Rowan shrugged.

'What do you think?' asked Sally.

'I don't know. A few months ago, I would've said she was paranoid, but now. . .' Rowan sighed and stared into space. She did not want to talk about this. To be honest, she was irritated with Eleanor. It should

129

have been a good evening. They had lit the stove and lounged in front of it, listening to music, toasting muffins and drinking fat mugs of hot chocolate – but Eleanor had flitted in and out of the room like a ghost, never quite staying, never quite going.

'I'm sorry if she ruined things, Sally.'

'It's not her fault she's jumpy. Besides, she didn't ruin anything. I had a great time.'

'Sometimes I wish we could be a bit more like you lot. Everything just seems to run off your backs. You don't let anything bother you.'

Sally sat up very straight in her bed. 'Of course things bother us!' she flared. 'Who do you think we are, a modern version of the Cratchitt family? Do you think Mum doesn't mind always struggling to pay the rent? Do you think the boys don't mind when they can't go to the multi-screen with their friends? Do you think it doesn't bother me, turning up at every party in the same T-shirt and jeans, when posers like Theresa would die rather than be seen in the same outfit twice?' Sally glared at Rowan before she settled back in bed.

'I'm really tired of it all, if you must know. I'm sick of never having enough money for anything and struggling to find the time to do my homework.'

'I'm sorry,' said Rowan, but Sally waved the apology away. She had moved on to a much bigger anger.

'We've got real problems, Rowan. Becky can't get a job, since she had Sam. They won't have her back where she used to work and no one else'll take the chance either. They all think she's going to have loads of time off whenever the baby's sick, even though she's told them she's living at home. And Mum can't do any more hours at the Baths, or they'll stop her benefit and we'll be worse off than we are now. So – I might have to take on full-time work at the super-market if things don't change soon.'

Rowan gasped at the thought of sharp, bright Sally stacking shelves all day. 'But what about your A levels?'

'I'll still get them. It'll just take me longer, that's all. I'll do evening classes at the college.' Sally yawned. 'It's all wrong though, isn't it?' she murmured sleepily. 'There's this – extra wall that women seem to have to climb over, especially if they want to be a bit different. Me and you, my mum, Becky, Eleanor. . . We're all just trying to make our way, aren't we? Just women trying to make our way. . .'

Sally was asleep, her anger forgotten. Her hands lay on top of the duvet, curled neatly, side by side, like rabbits' paws. The backs were covered with little raised lumps where the washing powder had irritated them. Rowan looked down at Sally lying in her exhausted sleep, and listened to Eleanor padding around the house checking the locks yet again. Suddenly her throat tightened with the strength of the connection she felt with them both. Just women, making our way, she thought.

Sally caught the first bus in to Bickersford on Sunday, refreshed and ready to spend the day on her French essay. Rowan walked to the stop with her through a fog so wet and heavy that beads of moisture condensed on all the curls in Sally's hair.

'Thanks,' she said. 'I needed that. See you at school tomorrow.'

Rowan waved her off and walked back to the barn. She was nearly at the door when a sudden gust of wind tore a hole in the fog and, just for an instant, she saw the brown car, parked over the road. Inside the car, a white smudge of a face turned towards her. Rowan felt her heart kick. She ran up to Eleanor, who was standing at the door waiting for her.

131

'Mum. That car—'

'I know. Come inside.'

'Are you going to phone the police?'

Eleanor's face creased with anxiety. 'After last time? I don't want to go jumping at shadows again. Maybe it's only coincidence. Maybe he did his shopping at the same time as us. Perhaps he's visiting someone over the road. I'll just keep an eye on things for now.'

She went to the window and peered out, but the fog pressed against the glass, as thick as mashed potatoes. Eleanor plunged her hands into the hot washing-up water and began to clear the breakfast dishes. Immediately, her anxious expression disappeared and her face became calm. Rowan looked at Eleanor's blank face and finally understood what the constant cleaning was about. Eleanor was using it as a sedative. The mindless activity was her way of forgetting.

Rowan watched, fascinated, until the washing-up was finished. As soon as the last spoon clattered into the drainer, Eleanor's face tightened. She glanced at the fog beyond the window and looked around for something else to do.

'Mum?' said Rowan, softly. 'I was going to do my homework over the road today. Do you want me to phone David and ask him over here instead?'

'David?'

'He – doesn't like being called IQ any more.'

'Oh, OK. Ask if Margaret wants to come over, will you?'

The women took over the kitchen, and Rowan and David sat together on the sofa in the main room, surrounded by textbooks. They were supposed to be working but Rowan could feel David gazing at her as she bent over the file on her knee.

'What?'

'I can't believe my luck,' he whispered.

'What about your essay?'

132

'I keep writing nonsense,' he breathed, leaning towards her. Rowan forgot all about her History essay as David slid his hands around her waist and pulled her close.

Something made her open her eyes in the middle of the kiss. She looked at the wall of glass and saw a face, looming out of the fog. It was a man's face and it was pressed against the bottom corner of the window, just in front of her feet. For a second, maybe two, she stared into his eyes. He had brown eyes. He was bald and skinny with a ratty face. He looked very cold.

'What's the matter?' asked David, breaking the kiss.

Rowan took a deep breath. 'There's a man watching us.'

David jumped up. The man let go of the terrace wall and fell out of sight into the field.

'Hey!' David yelled. He leapt for the terrace doors, flung them open, and hurdled the terrace wall.

'Wait!' screamed Rowan, but David had disappeared into the fog. 'There was a man – outside,' she cried, as Eleanor and Margaret came running in. 'David's gone after him.'

They all rushed into the road just in time to see the brown car roar past. The engine noise faded quickly, muffled by the swirling fog. There was no sign of David.

Margaret put her hands to her face. Rowan took a step forward.

'David?' she called. 'David?'

They all gasped when he stepped silently out of the fog and rushed past them into the kitchen.

'Are you all right?' asked Margaret, but David was chanting the car number plate over and over to himself and would not say anything until he had written it down on the message pad next to the phone.

'There,' he said. 'Call the police.'

* * *

133

'Don't worry,' said Inspector Duns. 'He's not connected with the idiots who did the paint job. And he's not dangerous – at least not in the way you're thinking. He's a private investigator.'

Eleanor's face turned bone white. Her eyes widened with shock. 'You mean – he's been spying on us?'

'Not very well by the sound of it. Salinger is useless at surveillance. What he is good at though, is digging up dirt – or anything that can be turned into dirt. A lot of the defence barristers use him, in rape and sexual assault cases, to try to weaken the woman's case. Warn your friends. He's probably going to be snooping around asking a lot of questions.'

'He can't go round looking through people's back windows like that,' fumed Rowan. 'Can't you arrest him?'

'Was he actually standing on the terrace, Rowan?' asked Inspector Duns.

'No. He was peering over the wall right up against the house.'

'Is that your field, Mrs Fletcher?'

Eleanor shook her head. 'It belongs to the farmer.'

'Then I'm afraid you can't do a thing about it. You can't even get him for trespass. If it's any consolation, all this is costing Mason an awful lot of money. Now, if his defence team have hired Salinger, it sounds to me as though they're on their final push. They must've heard before we did.'

'What? What have they heard?'

'We've been lucky. A couple of charges withdrawn, a mis-trial. We've got a much earlier slot in the Crown Court schedule than we were expecting.'

'When?' said Eleanor, gripping the table top.

'Eight weeks' time. We go to court in the New Year.'

Two

Eleanor stopped cleaning the terrace windows. She screened the corners with piles of books and turned the chairs and sofa around, so that they faced into the room instead of out to the valley. Still, she was not happy. She frowned up at the bright expanse of glass and called in glaziers and builders, who tramped through the barn in their heavy boots and talked about fitting blinds or mirror glass.

'Why do we need these?' demanded Rowan, flicking at the pile of estimates. 'You used to love those windows.'

'I know. But that was when I thought they were for us to look out of, not for others to look in. Anyway,' said Eleanor, pushing the estimates into the back of a kitchen drawer. 'I'm not going to do anything yet. These quotes are all so expensive.'

As the days grew colder and shorter, and the trial date drew nearer, Eleanor forgot about the windows. A new worry began to obsess her. 'I feel so unprepared,' she said. 'How can I walk into that courtroom knowing nothing about what's going to happen?'

'Why don't you ask Inspector Duns?' said Rowan.

'I have. He just tells me not to worry. He says all I have to do is to tell the court what I told him. That's not enough for me, sweetheart. I need – more.'

135

Rowan got up and unpinned a slip of paper from the top corner of the kitchen notice board. It was the telephone number of the local Rape Crisis Centre. Margaret had brought it over one day in the summer, and it had been there ever since. 'What about giving these people a try?' she said.

Rowan was attempting to make a flan when the volunteer arrived from the Rape Crisis Centre.

'Hello, Mrs Fletcher,' said a horribly familiar voice when Eleanor opened the door. 'I'm Eva. We've met before, at the school.'

Conrad the Barbarian! For a moment, Rowan was convinced that the Domestic Science teacher must be doing a spot check for untidy work surfaces and she stared down at the messy kitchen bench in a panic. Eva Conrad did, in fact, wag her finger at the clutter of flour, eggshells and grated cheese when she saw it.

'Didn't I teach you to clear up as you went along?' she said, peering into the bowl of fat and flour which the recipe book said had to be rubbed to a 'breadcrumb consistency'.

'More speed, more lift!' she cried, watching Rowan's fumbling fingers.

'Yes, miss,' said Rowan, instantly transported back to the Year Seven Domestic Science class.

'So, where do you want to talk?' asked Eva, giving up on Rowan and turning to face Eleanor. Rowan gave a sigh of relief. Of course, Eva Conrad wasn't checking up on her! What a ridiculous idea. She was the volunteer. Rowan became very still then, as she remembered what Eleanor had told her about the volunteer. Apparently she was a real expert on court procedure because she had been through it all herself, which meant – which meant that, at some time in her life, Conrad the Barbarian had been attacked, too, just like Eleanor. Rowan's hands clenched in the pastry mix as the shock ran through her.

'Let's sit in here,' said Eleanor. Rowan heard the kitchen chairs scrape behind her as the two women settled down.

'What have the police told you, Mrs Fletcher?'

'Please, call me Eleanor. The police haven't said anything, really, except not to worry.'

'Yes. They're frightened in case you decide to drop the charges, that's why they're not telling you much. A lot of women do drop the charges, you see, after the police have done all the work setting up the case. It's a problem for them. So, what do you want to know?'

'Everything. I want to go into court knowing exactly what's going to happen.'

Eva Conrad took a deep breath. 'All right. First of all, you might be wondering why you don't have a lawyer. That's because the police are bringing the case, not you. You're only their main witness. You're not even allowed to talk to the prosecution barrister, because that barrister could then be accused of telling a witness what to say before she takes the stand. On the other hand, your attacker has had a whole team of defence lawyers working on his case since the day he was charged. No one knows what his defence is going to be, but his lawyers know everything about the police case. They've seen all the statements, including yours. So, you should ask to see your statement again before the trial – and you need to have every detail of what happened clear in your head when you go into the witness box.'

'What happens, when I take the stand?'

'The prosecution or police case is always heard first. They have to present all their witnesses, starting with you. You are the most important witness, so you could be in the box for anything from two days to a week, at a guess. First of all the prosecution barrister gets you to tell the jury what happened. After that, your attacker's barrister is allowed to cross-examine you. That's your bit over then. The rest of the police witnesses take the stand, then the case for the defence starts. The same thing happens, but the other way round. The defence witnesses appear, including your attacker if he chooses to take the stand, and the prosecution barrister gets to cross-examine them.'

'There'll be plenty of defence witnesses,' said Eleanor. 'The whole of his Theatre Group will be fighting to get out there and tell everyone how wonderful he is.'

'After that, the two barristers deliver their final speeches, the judge sums up the whole thing and the jury go off to reach their verdict. Is there anything you want to ask about that?'

'Jeff Mason. Will he be there, when I have to talk about the attack?'

'Yes, I'm afraid so. He'll be sitting in the dock for the whole of the trial. But try not to worry about him. Your biggest enemy in that court room is not him, it's his defence barrister.' Eva Conrad hesitated. When she spoke again, her voice was no longer cool and neutral but full of a painful intensity. 'Look, you need to know this. You need to be prepared. The job of the defence barrister is to create doubt in the minds of the jury, and he's going to do that in any way he can. He's going to do his best to show that you are a liar and a woman who cannot be trusted. He is an expert at turning everything on its head, and he's going to use dirty tricks you won't even have dreamed of. If there is anything in your past he can use against you, he will. He won't care about you or your feelings. It's his job to be ruthless.'

There was a long silence, then. Rowan glared down into her pastry bowl, waiting for Eleanor to speak.

'Sounds like it's going to be tough,' said Eleanor, finally. Her voice shook. 'Could I drop the charges – even now?'

'Yes, if that's what you want.'

There was another long pause, then Eleanor said, 'What are my chances, if I go ahead?'

'You've done very well to get this far,' Eva Conrad said, carefully. 'A lot of women can't even face reporting an attack. Of the ones that do go to the police, only about a quarter of them get as far as going to court.'

'But what are my chances of getting a guilty verdict?'

Eva hesitated. 'The odds are against you. You see, the jury has to be sure the man is guilty beyond any reasonable doubt. That's the law. So, all the defence barrister has to do is to create doubt, to confuse the jury, in any way he can.

'There's another thing you need to know about. This is the law too, although there's a big campaign going on to get it changed. There's something the judge has to say to the jury in every rape and sexual assault case.'

'What?'

'The judge has to tell the jury that sometimes women who claim to have been attacked are not telling the truth—'

'He says what!'

'I know. I know it sounds bad. The judge has to tell them that and remind them that they mustn't convict just on what the woman says.'

'But – that's outrageous!'

'It's the law. The trouble is, the jury doesn't realize that the judge always has to say that. Your jury will think he's saying it about you and your evidence.

They'll think the judge doesn't believe you. Put that together with the "guilty beyond any reasonable doubt" idea, and you can see why a jury doesn't often come up with a guilty verdict for rape or sexual assault. I'm sorry. But it's best to know before you go in there, so you can be prepared. Here.'

Rowan heard the rip as Eva Conrad tore off a piece of kitchen roll, and she knew Eleanor must be crying. Her own tears were dripping from her chin and making craters in the smooth surface of the flour on the bench.

'What will you do, Eleanor?'

'I've got no choice, really. I have to go on with it. How can I withdraw the charges now? Everyone would think I'd been lying about the whole thing.'

'I know how you feel,' said Eva Conrad. 'Just remember, when you get into that witness box, it's all a show. They're all performing out there, trying to make the jury see things their way. You've got to do the same. Treat it like a performance and do everything you can to make it a convincing one. Everything counts. What you wear, how you talk. You've got to be ruthless, too. Don't be decent and reasonable, or the defence barrister is going to walk all over you. You've got to fight him all the way!'

Eleanor looked at Eva Conrad and asked, 'Can you tell me, did you win your case?'

'No. I lost. I was raped twenty years ago, by the husband of the woman I was babysitting for. He offered me a lift home, but he stopped the car halfway there and attacked me. I reported it right away and took him to court, but his lawyers got him off on the consent issue. He said I'd agreed to sex and only got upset afterwards when I realized how late home I was going to be. He said I made up the rape story so my parents wouldn't be angry with me for being so late. Reasonable doubt, you see.'

Eleanor shook her head. 'Where does justice come into all this?'

The chair scraped again as Eva Conrad stood up. She walked over to Rowan and touched her on the shoulder.

'Rowan, you know you mustn't tell a soul at school about this, don't you?'

'Oh, no, I won't tell anyone, Miss Conrad. Never!' said Rowan, spinning to face her. Eva Conrad smiled and touched her wet cheek.

'Good girl.' She peered into the pastry bowl and raised her eyebrows. Rowan looked down too, and realized that she had squashed the mixture into a hard, grey ball.

'Oops,' she said.

'I hope it turns out well,' said Eva Conrad, as she slipped out of the door.

'Did she mean the pastry, or the trial?' asked Rowan, genuinely confused.

Eleanor spluttered behind her square of kitchen roll and Rowan looked at her in surprise.

'Don't laugh,' she said, pretending to be offended. 'God, that really shook me up, her coming in when I was trying to make something.'

Eleanor snorted and put down the tissue. 'Your face was a picture when she walked in and started. . .' Eleanor began to shake with laughter, even though the tears were still running down her cheeks.

'More speed, more lift!' yelled Rowan, feeling the tension seep from the room. 'If you knew the number of times I heard that in cookery lessons.' She shook her head at Eleanor who was, by now, doubled up in her chair. 'We all used to march around the yard afterwards, copying her. "More speed, more lift! More speed, more lift!" '

She picked up the grey lump from the bowl and

141

slapped it on the table in front of Eleanor. 'What do you think?' she asked. 'Doesn't that look tasty?'

They leaned together, hooting uncontrollably.

'Why are we laughing,' gasped Eleanor, when she could talk, 'after what we've just heard?'

'I don't know,' said Rowan. 'I think we needed to. I think we would've exploded otherwise.'

They stared at one another solemnly for a few seconds. Then the pastry lump keeled over onto the kitchen table with a wet splat and set them off again.

The morning of the first day of the trial was cold and full of heavy grey clouds, promising snow. Rowan made tea and toast automatically, even though she felt as though her stomach was lined with concrete. When Eleanor came down, she stared. She couldn't help it. Eleanor was wearing a matching navy skirt and jacket, with a white blouse underneath. Her hair was pulled up into a bun and she tapped across the kitchen floor in discreet black shoes with small heels.

'Mum! Why are you dressed like that?'

'Like what?'

'You know. You look like – like Margaret.'

'What's wrong with looking like Margaret?'

'Nothing, if you are Margaret. But those things aren't you—'

'Now, don't start. You know what Eva said. It's all a show and I have to present myself in a way the jury find acceptable.'

'But Mum, you look—'

'Rowan!' Eleanor's voice cracked dangerously.

'—fine. You look fine. Let me come with you. Please?'

'Sweetheart, we've been through this so many

142

times. I just want to get it over with as quietly as possible and I want you to stay right out of it. It's a dirty business, the whole thing, and I don't want you involved. Now here comes Margaret, look. I have to go. I'll see you tonight. Don't worry. I don't want you to worry.'

They hugged, then stepped back and nodded at one another, wordlessly, their faces fierce with held-back tears. Eleanor grabbed her coat and walked off down the path beside Margaret, without looking back.

When they had driven off, Rowan began to collect her own things together, desperate to get over the road to David. She reached into the drawer for a pair of gloves and her hand closed around Eleanor's blue scarf. Rowan pulled it out and buried her face in the soft wool. The scarf still carried the scent of Eleanor's favourite perfume, the one she wouldn't wear any more. Rowan breathed in the smell of Eleanor then, on an impulse, stuffed the scarf into her pocket and raced out of the barn. David was waiting for her at his front door and she ran into his arms and burst into tears.

'Come on,' he said, leading her through to the living room at the back of the house. 'I've got the fire lit in here.' He guided her to the sofa and gave her his handkerchief. She let him take her coat and gloves away but, when he tried to take the blue scarf, she clutched it tight.

'No, don't take that. It's Mum's.'

'Oh, OK,' said David, sitting beside her and putting his arm around her shoulders.

'I just feel as though I want to hang on to this, today,' said Rowan, stroking the blue scarf. 'It reminds me what Mum used to be like. If I hang on to this, maybe everything'll go well today. Maybe I'll get her back again. It's stupid, really. Kid's stuff. Like not stepping on the cracks. Remember that?'

143

' "Step on a crack, break your mother's back," ' smiled David. 'I remember. What was that other thing we used to do? If you saw a cat, you had to hop until you saw a dog, or you'd die of some horrible illness.'

'I remember! And the ghost curtains, remember them? We had to get past that empty house without the wind moving the curtains in the broken window. If the curtains moved while we were still running past, that meant the ghost would come to get us.'

David laughed. 'We'd all be stuck there for ages on a windy day, trying to get past. We used to scare ourselves silly, didn't we? And some of the stuff we got up to was really dangerous, too. Remember the live-for-ever pipe?'

Rowan nodded, picturing the fat, metal sewage pipe, which emerged from the river bank just above the weir and bridged the water, before burying itself in the opposite bank again. One summer, when they were ten, a whole gang of them made that stretch of river their base. They had been playing in the shallows one day, making dams and catching sticklebacks, when Sally called out somewhere above them. Rowan could still remember the way her shrill voice had pierced the rumble of the weir.

'Hey!'

They had looked up to see Sally standing on top of the pipe. 'If you can walk all the way across,' she called, 'then you'll live for ever and ever!' She had danced across, above the sparkling water, laughing all the way.

'I dare you!' she yelled from the other side and they had gone to join her, one by one. Even little Gary managed it, by edging across on all fours, and Rowan had been left on the bank, alone.

As she stepped out onto the slippery curved metal, Rowan forgot about living for ever. Instead, she thought about dying very soon, but she shuffled forward anyway, keeping her eyes on her friends across the river. She reached the join between the first and second sections of pipe without once lifting her feet. There, she had stopped and stared down at the raised lip of metal with the streaks of rust fanning out from each rivet. She was stuck. Her feet had refused to leave the pipe and step over the join.

'Remember the way we all balanced across?' said David.

'Not all of us. I was the only one who couldn't do it,' frowned Rowan. 'I had to shuffle off the stupid thing backwards because I was too scared to turn round.'

'But I did it for you,' smiled David. 'Had you forgotten? They said I had to run because I was doing it for someone else, so it had to be more difficult. Don't you remember?'

'Yes!' gasped Rowan, sitting up straight on the sofa as the memory came flooding back. There he was! Racing towards her across the pipe as though it was as wide and flat as a runway. With his arms stretched wide for balance and his skinny legs flying across the sunlit metal, he defied gravity and death. A boy made of air and light.

It was dark when they heard the key in the lock. Rowan stood up, clutching the scarf, as Margaret and Eleanor came into the room.

'How was it?' she asked, looking at Eleanor's white face.

'Pathetic!' snapped Margaret. 'Talk about bad organization. We spent most of the day stuck in this little waiting room. Very cheerful that was, with no windows and hard chairs, and these huge old heating pipes running around the walls. First, they spent the morning hearing other pleas. Then they broke for

145

lunch. Then they had to swear the jury in and weed out a couple and swear in a couple of spares. That took most of the afternoon. By the time they called your mum to the stand, the day was nearly over. She'd only just got started when the judge decided it was time for his tea!'

'Mum? What was it like?'

Eleanor stared into the fire. 'Climbing up the steps into the witness box, that was the worst bit. The court was packed. All the lawyers and the clerks and the judge and the jury and the court officials. And him.' Eleanor shuddered. 'The public gallery was full, too.'

'And most of them were his friends,' interrupted Margaret. 'All those women from the Theatre Group in the front row seats, tutting and huffing and laughing at what your mum was saying. They were just like those women who took their knitting along to watch the guillotine in the French Revolution—'

'And tomorrow, I've got to stand there and talk about the attack, with him staring at me. . .' Eleanor clamped her hands together and closed her eyes.

'I'll make a cup of tea,' said Margaret.

'No. No thanks. I think I just want to get home, Margaret. Home and safe and quiet.'

Eleanor and Rowan scurried across the road, heads bent against the icy wind, intent on getting into the barn. They squeezed between parked cars onto the pavement and hurried up to the front door. Eleanor had her key halfway to the lock when all the car doors opened behind them.

'Mrs Fletcher?'

They turned and flinched as flash bulbs went off all around them, peppering the darkness with explosions of white light.

'Oh! I dropped my key!' said Eleanor, falling to her knees and scrabbling for her key ring as the reporters surged towards them. Rowan fell back against the wall of the barn as they surrounded Eleanor.

'How did the first day go, Mrs Fletcher? How do you feel?'

'People are saying you're making this up. Want to give us your side of the story?'

'No comment,' Eleanor said, plucking her key from under the feet of the scrum.

'Mrs Fletcher, Eleanor. The college is backing Jeff Mason and it seems he has a lot of support in the town. How do you feel about that?'

'No comment,' shouted Eleanor, forcing her way through to the door and struggling to slot her key into the lock.

'Is it true that you actually went away with him for the weekend?'

'No comment!' She flung open the door and pushed Rowan inside. 'Go away and leave us alone!' she cried, swinging back to face the reporters. Her arm caught the camera of the man nearest the door and it fell to the frozen ground with a dull thud.

'Hey!' he yelled, picking it up and cradling it like a baby. 'If you can't stand the heat, lady, you should stay out of the kitchen!'

Eleanor slammed the door and they leaned against it, clinging together, as the reporters rattled the letter box and banged on the window. After several minutes, it suddenly went quiet, except for the ragged catch of their breathing.

'I think they've given up,' whispered Rowan. She raised her head. The dark shapes at the window had gone. Quickly, she pulled down the blinds and put on the light. Eleanor was still crouched by the door.

'Come on, Mum,' said Rowan, lifting her by the elbows and guiding her to a chair. 'You're going to get your smart suit all creased.'

Rowan was shaking all over, but she tried to stay

calm for Eleanor. She moved around the kitchen, bolting the door, turning the heating up and putting the kettle on to boil. The familiar noises seemed to get through to Eleanor. Slowly, she straightened up. Some colour came back to her cheeks.

'All right?'

Eleanor nodded and stood up. 'I'll take that,' she said, picking up the loaded tea tray. 'Let's get into the back, out of the way.'

Rowan opened the door to the main room and Eleanor walked past her with the tray. A second later, the tea things crashed to the floor as the wall of glass in front of them splintered into starbursts of light. Rowan hit the light switch and the pack of reporters became visible, crowding against the terrace windows. Hands, faces and camera lenses loomed out of the darkness, pressing against the glass. The fists knocked and the eyes glared into the barn. The mouths opened, letting out muffled shouts and white plumes of breath.

'Mrs Fletcher! Mrs Fletcher, tell us about the attack. Did he tie you up? Did he hurt you? Did you struggle?'

Eleanor turned and ran for the bathroom, slipping in the pool of tea as she went. Rowan followed, slamming the door after her.

'Our house! Looking into our house!' Rowan was outraged. 'They were standing on our terrace!' She stopped, remembering something Inspector Duns had said. 'We can get them for trespass, Mum.'

Eleanor shook her head. 'It would take months and anyway their newspapers would pay the fines for them. Meanwhile, they've got their photographs for tomorrow's papers. They've got what they wanted. Oh, Rowan, I'm so sorry! I've been such a fool, getting us into this. I should never have started it.'

'You didn't start it, Mum. He did.'

'But I'm the one everyone's out to get. You heard

those reporters out there. It seems like the real crime is bringing it out in the open.'

'Mum!' Rowan grabbed Eleanor's hands and held them in hers. 'Don't say that. Listen, he's the criminal and he's going to get punished.' She squeezed Eleanor's hands but they lay cold and limp in her palms, like little fish.

'No. I should've remembered,' said Eleanor. 'He always wins.' Rowan pulled her hands away, shivering at the echo of Paul Mason's warning. She looked down at her mother and Eleanor stared back, her face full of a dull certainty.

'I'm going to lose.'

Late that night, Rowan was woken by the sound of hammering. All the lights were on in the main room. She crawled out of bed and padded out onto the gallery. Eleanor had collected together every spare sheet and blanket in the barn and dumped them in a pile in front of the terrace windows. She was at the top of the stepladder now, struggling to stretch a tartan travel rug across one of the windows and nail it to the wooden frame.

Rowan nearly went downstairs to help, but something about the dull, defeated way Eleanor was moving made her hold back. Eleanor had been moving that way since the moment in the bathroom when she said she was going to lose. It was as though she was sedated. Rowan bit her lip. Of all the changes Eleanor had been through since the attack, this nothingness was the worst of all. This was so far away from the old Eleanor that, for the first time, Rowan thought she might never come back. The thought made Rowan so frightened, she could not look at her mother any longer. She went back to her room and softly closed the door.

MY BOSS GAVE ME
MORE THAN A LECTURE
Tutor Alleges Sex Attack On
Weekend Away

Jeffrey Mason, Head of Department at Bickersford College, spent his second day in court yesterday, accused of attempting to rape one of his tutors on a weekend residential course.

Dark-haired divorcée, Eleanor Fletcher, had previously told the court of her surprise at being invited on the weekend. The thirty-nine year old drama tutor described her professional relationship with her forty-six year old boss as 'cool' since she had fought to stop him cutting one of her most popular courses.

'I thought asking me on the weekend was his way of making a new start, but it soon emerged that the invitation was not his idea. He did not want me there at all,' said the petite, attractive college lecturer who claims that her boss subjected her to a catalogue of humiliations and insults from the moment she arrived at the country hotel.

Upset

Mrs Fletcher became visibly upset when she had to describe the alleged attack. She claimed that Mr Mason followed her into an empty coffee bar, threw her to the floor and restrained her by wrapping her skirt around her arms and head. He allegedly indecently assaulted her and was about to rape her when a cleaner disturbed him by banging on the door, which he had locked upon entering the room.

He Was Out To Hurt Me

When asked by Mr John Elliot QC why she thought Mr Mason had attacked her, Mrs Fletcher replied, 'He was in such a rage. It was a way of hurting me. It had nothing to do with sex.'

The trial continues today, when Mrs Fletcher faces cross-examination by Mr Carver QC, one of the most hard-hitting defence barristers on the circuit.

Rowan threw the paper down to join the others littering Margaret's carpet. Eleanor stared out of every page. Each photograph had captured a different slice of the scuffle outside the barn, but her look of wide-eyed shock was the same in every one of them.

'They'll have forgotten this by next week,' said David.

'Who?'

'The people who read the tabloids. The Great British Public. They've got the memory of a goldfish where news is concerned. Do you know how long that is?'

'What?'

'A goldfish's memory. No? Three and a half seconds. That's why it's not cruel to keep a goldfish in a bowl. It swims around, past its little plaster castle and it says to itself, "That's a nice castle." Then, the next time it swims round, it gives a jump of surprise and says, "My goodness, what a pretty castle." See? It never gets bored, because it can only remember the last three and a half seconds. . .'

Rowan looked up from the newspapers with a puzzled frown. 'What?'

'Doesn't matter,' sighed David. 'Forget it. So. Day

151

three. What shall we do today? Do you think you could face school?'

Rowan shook her head.

'OK. We could go over to the barn.'

'No. Mum has arranged for some workmen to come in today, to put up blinds or something on the terrace windows.'

'Another day here, then,' said David, looking around the little back room with a slightly trapped expression.

'No,' Rowan decided, standing up. 'I'm going to court.'

The Crown Court building stood on a hill above the old city centre like an inside-out wedding cake. The outer walls were brown and crumbly but, when Rowan and David walked through the arched doorway, they found an entrance hall and stairwell iced with elaborate white plasterwork.

'Which court?' whispered David.

'Three.'

He veered towards a small door with a sign above it saying, 'Public Gallery, Number 3 Court' and Rowan followed. Their footsteps clacked on the marble floor and echoed in the high, domed roof as they crossed the hall. Rowan dug her fingers into David's arm.

'That security man's watching us.'

'It's all right,' he murmured. 'No one's interested in us. We're just two law students from the university, right? Act confident.'

The door swung open silently, and they slipped through. The skin on Rowan's back tightened as she waited for the security man to shout, but the door sighed shut again behind them. She gulped in some air and looked around. They were standing in a dark cubby hole at the bottom of a narrow staircase. When

152

Rowan looked up to the top of the staircase, she could see more icing columns supporting another domed ceiling.

A man was talking in the courtroom. His voice was loud and assured. The domed ceiling amplified his words and sent them rolling around the courtroom. Mr Carver, QC, thought Rowan.

'Very well, Ms Fletcher,' said Mr Carver, lingering over the Ms. 'Let us move away, for the moment, from the details of the alleged attack. Let us put to one side the bruises on your arms which nobody else saw, and the green velvet dress, which cannot be examined for signs of rough treatment because you – threw it away.' His voice rose, high with disbelief.

'Let us move on to the time lapse between the alleged attack and the complaint you submitted to the college over a week later. Can you tell the jury why you did not report this alleged attack immediately?'

A pause. Then Rowan heard Eleanor's voice rising up from the well of the courtroom. 'I – I was too upset to talk about it to start with.'

Rowan squeezed her eyes shut and bit on the knuckles of one hand. 'I can't,' she whispered to David, and turned to leave.

A disembodied head in a white wig loomed out of the darkness beside them. 'Court is in session,' hissed a woman, bringing her hands out of her black gown for a second to frown at her watch. She was wearing a badge with the word 'USHER' printed on it.

'Sorry,' whispered David. 'Law seminar ran late.' He grabbed Rowan's hand and they tiptoed away from the usher, up the stairs and into the courtroom.

Three

The staircase came out at the back of the gallery. Tiers of semi-circular benches sloped down towards the floor of the courtroom like the balcony seats in a theatre.

All a show, thought Rowan as she and David slid quietly onto the end of the back bench, which was hard, narrow and covered in slippery red leather. Rowan kept her head tucked inside her coat collar in case someone turned to look up at them, but the other people in the gallery were intent on the scene below. Most of the Theatre Group were there, sitting in the two front rows, and Margaret had planted herself squarely in the middle of them, with her elbows out and her coat and bags spread out on the bench either side of her.

Rowan relaxed a little and sat up to see over the edge of the gallery. Eleanor was standing in the witness box to the left of the judge and facing the jury. She was the only person standing in the whole of the courtroom. She looked tiny and frightened, like a little girl who had been caught playing dressing-up games in her mother's smartest clothes. Rowan's heart ached.

'Ms Fletcher. Is it true that you did not submit your complaint to the college until after you had read

Mr Mason's report on your unprofessional conduct during the weekend?'

'Well, I couldn't—'

'Just answer the question please!'

'Yes, that is true. But—'

'Thank you. Is it not also true that you initially gave food poisoning as the reason for your absence from work after the weekend?'

'I told you, I couldn't talk about the real—'

'Yes or no!' roared Mr Carver, leaving the shadow of the gallery and surging towards the witness box like a great black shark. Rowan got her first look at him. He was a big, red-faced man who should have looked ridiculous in his white wig with the sausages of rolled-up hair at each side and the little black bow at the back. Instead he brimmed with confidence and anger.

Down in the witness box, Eleanor flinched.

'Yes,' she whispered. 'I said I had food poisoning.'

'And the food poisoning story was a lie, was it not?'

'Yes.'

Up in the gallery, the Theatre Group tutted and muttered, loud enough for the jury to hear.

'Yes! You lied, Ms Fletcher! And if you lied then, how can the jury be sure that you are telling the truth now?'

Mr Carver turned to the jury and spread his arms before walking back under the gallery, out of Rowan's field of vision. She knew Jeff Mason must be under there, in the dock, even though she could not see him. She knew because Eleanor's gaze kept skipping past that space under the gallery, refusing to look.

'Ms Fletcher. Would you say you were good at putting on an act?'

'I don't understand. . .'

'You specialize in Drama, do you not?'

155

'Yes, but Drama is the opposite of putting on an act. Theatre is about putting on an act. Drama is about finding truths.'

'Very well, let me put it another way. You are an accomplished actress, Ms Fletcher. In fact you won a prize recently, did you not?'

'Not just me. The whole of my drama group. We won the prize for best production at this year's festival.'

'Quite so. Tell the court about your production, Ms Fletcher.'

Rowan bit her lip, suddenly realizing where the questioning was leading.

'It grew out of an improvisation we did about how girls and women are expected to behave in society—'

'What was your part in this?' Mr Carver interrupted.

'The play was based on the case of a real girl who was found living wild in the woods like an animal. I played the wolf girl and the others played the various experts all ready to give their opinions on how she should be civilized.'

'How were you dressed for this part?'

'Well, my hair was all tangled. I was covered in dirt—'

'You were naked, were you not, Ms Fletcher?'

There was an audible intake of breath from the jury. Pens began to scribble in the press box.

'No!' protested Eleanor, finally realizing where the defence barrister was heading. 'I wore a flesh-coloured body stocking. I was not naked—'

'You were, in the eyes of the audience, naked!' roared Mr Carver, stalking towards the witness box.

'I was meant to look naked, yes, but it wasn't a – a sexual thing. I looked like a filthy savage creature, covered in dirt—'

'Ms Fletcher!' roared the QC, grabbing the edge of

156

the box as though he was about to climb in and shake the answer out of Eleanor. 'Did you or did you not appear, on stage, in front of an audience, in effect, naked!'

'Objection,' drawled the prosecution barrister, half getting to his feet, then slumping back in his chair.

'Mr Carver,' said the judge. 'What do you hope to prove with this line of questioning?'

'Your Honour, I merely wish to show that the witness is, as I said, an accomplished actress. It is relevant to the case.'

'Hmmm. Move on.'

Mr Carver bowed his head. He had achieved what he had set out to do. Rowan could see the way the jurors were looking at Eleanor now, especially the women.

'Very well,' said Mr Carver. 'Let us move on to your hotel room. The room was left in such a mess that the police are using it as evidence of your state of mind when you walked out halfway through the weekend. They even have a collection of various oddments which you left behind. They say you must have been dreadfully upset to leave your room like that. Yes?'

Eleanor nodded and the judge leaned towards her, his long wig swinging forward like a poodle's ears. 'Please give a verbal answer, Mrs Fletcher, for the court records.'

'Yes. I was so distressed, I don't even remember packing my bag.'

'Ms Fletcher, did you write this?'

Eleanor took the college magazine from Mr Carver with shaking hands and looked at the page. Her head shot up again and her face was full of a desperate understanding.

'This was a joke! It's not meant to be serious!'

Up in the gallery, Rowan strained forward on the

bench. Her hands were clenched so tightly together, the knuckles were white, but she did not notice. She was down in the box with Eleanor, backing up every word her mother said.

'Did you write that article?'

'Yes—'

'Read the title to the court.'

Eleanor looked at the prosecution barrister, but he showed no sign of objecting again. She bent her head to the magazine. ' "Confessions of a total slut," ' she read.

'The total slut being you, Ms Fletcher?'

'Yes.'

'And the first line?'

Eleanor lowered the magazine and looked at Mr Carver. 'This is not a serious article—'

'The first line, please.'

'I hate tidy rooms—'

' "I hate tidy rooms!" ' Mr Carver whipped out his own copy of the magazine and strode over to the jury box. 'Ms Fletcher goes on to write, "I am never comfortable unless I am surrounded by mess. Mess means that something more creative than dusting has been taking place. People with tidy houses usually have empty minds.'

'You seem to have a very low opinion of us ordinary people, Ms Fletcher,' said Mr Carver, instantly allying himself and the jury against her.

'It was a joke!' cried Eleanor.

'I put it to you, Ms Fletcher, that the state of your room did not reflect your state of mind. I suggest that you left your hotel room in a mess because you are, in your own words, a slut!'

'No! I was devastated!'

'Or maybe – angry?'

Eleanor frowned, thrown by the sudden change of tack. 'No,' she said slowly. 'Not angry.'

Mr Carver drew himself up and hooked his thumbs into the lapels of his black gown. His voice rang out, full of conviction. 'I suggest that you, in fact, abandoned your room and your professional commitments that weekend in a fit of anger after Mr Mason resisted your attempts to seduce him in the coffee bar!'

There was a second of stunned silence, then an excited buzz ran through the spectators in the public gallery.

'No!' cried Eleanor, her face gaunt with shock.

'Oh, yes, Ms Fletcher. That was what really happened, was it not? My client did follow you to the coffee bar, I accept that much, but only to inform you that he felt bound to report your lateness, your lack of preparation and your totally unprofessional attitude to the college on his return. It was you, Ms Fletcher, who locked the coffee room door, when you realized that my client was not to be dissuaded from reporting you. You locked the door and attempted to seduce my client as a way of weakening his resolve!'

'Oh, that is such a lie—'

'And then, when my client refused your advances, you told him that if he went ahead with his complaint to the college, you would blacken his name with an accusation of attempted rape, didn't you, Ms Fletcher?'

'No! None of that is true!'

'Are we supposed to take your word for that, Ms Fletcher? We have already established that you lied to your employers about the food poisoning. We have also established that you are good at putting on an act and that you are not afraid to use – to display – your body. You are not some shrinking spinster, Ms Fletcher. You are a divorced woman with an active social and sexual life.'

159

'No,' said Eleanor, in a strong, clear voice. 'I have not had a sexual relationship since my husband left.'

Mr Carver turned to the jury and raised his eyebrows in a pantomime of disbelief. 'Ms Fletcher, remember you are on oath here. Are you telling me that you, a young, attractive woman, have not had a single sexual relationship in fourteen long years?'

'I could have had relationships. I chose not to. I decided to make my daughter my companion until she left home. I felt I owed it to her. I wanted to be more than a mother to her since her father was not there.'

Rowan stared down at Eleanor, astonished. She had never thought about the lack of men friends before. What would her mother want with men friends? She had her, didn't she? For the first time, Rowan looked at Eleanor and saw more than her mother. She saw a woman who had made a hard decision.

'Aha. So, Ms Fletcher, you are now telling us that you are devoted to your daughter? Would you say you were – a good mother?' Mr Carver's voice was bland, but Eleanor was a fast learner. She hesitated, looking for the hidden trap.

'Yes,' she said, finally.

'Would you say that you always put your daughter's interests first?'

'Yes,' said Eleanor. 'I do.'

Up in the gallery, Rowan unwittingly nodded agreement.

'Yet you agreed to be a tutor on this course in the full knowledge that you would be leaving your daughter alone in the house for a whole weekend.'

'That's not true. I agreed only because I knew I could arrange for my daughter to stay with a good friend of mine.'

'You may have planned to make such arrangements,' said Mr Carver. 'But that is not what actually happened, is it?'

Rowan was stunned. How could he know that she had stayed in the barn on her own? The private investigator must have found out somehow. But who would tell him . . .? Theresa! Theresa must have talked to Salinger. That was the only explanation. Rowan clenched her fists and glared down at the QC.

'You did, in fact, leave your young daughter to fend for herself on that weekend, didn't you, Ms Fletcher?'

'Yes,' said Eleanor softly, looking down at her hands. It was obvious that she felt guilty. Rowan groaned. My fault, she thought. I should've stayed with Margaret. Why did I insist on staying on my own when she wasn't happy with it?

Eleanor pulled herself together and raised her head. 'When my daughter asked to stay at home and look after herself, I agreed, even though I would have preferred her to stay with my friend. My daughter is very mature for her age and she is old enough to stay on her own. I did ask my friend to keep an eye on things for me.'

'I see.' Mr Carver bowed his head and walked to the witness box. 'Ms Fletcher,' he said, quietly, almost confidentially. 'You claim to be a good mother, yet you leave your daughter at home alone. You claim to be a good employee, made to look incompetent by my client – yet you admit to staying away from work and lying to your employers. I wonder,' he said, his voice rising to a shout, 'do you ever open your mouth without telling a lie!'

The prosecution lawyer clambered to his feet. 'Objection.'

'Do you, Ms Fletcher?'

'Objection!'

Eleanor broke down then, sobbing into her cupped hands. Rowan slid from the bench and clattered down the stairs, unable to stay another second.

* * *

161

They only spoke once on the bus from the city back to Bickersford.

'She's the most honest person I know,' said Rowan.

'Of course she is,' said David, beside her. 'That man could make Gandhi look bad.'

The bus passed through busy city streets, then suburbs full of houses to reach the old Roman road that ran, straight as an arrow, between the city and Bickersford. Rowan stared out at all the people shopping or cycling, painting their houses or washing their cars. She watched them with the same surprise she had felt when she looked out of the window of the black limousine on the way to her grandma's funeral. How could all this ordinary life still be going on, when her life had turned into a disaster?

'I need to get some essay notes from school,' said David, when they climbed down from the bus in Bickersford. 'I'll be in real trouble next week, if I don't. What about waiting for me in the library? I'll only be five minutes.'

Rowan shook her head. 'No. I'll get home. Warm the place up and get some dinner ready.'

'OK. I'll come with you,' said David, crossing the road to the bus stop with her.

'What, and then have to go back down the hill to school afterwards? No. That would be silly. Go and get your essay notes. I'll be fine.'

'I don't know. . .'

'I'll phone you, this evening,' said Rowan, stretching up to kiss his cheek.

She watched him lope off down the street with his jacket collar turned up against the bitter wind. When he reached the corner, he turned to wave before disappearing along the school road. Rowan huddled into her own collar and stamped her feet, willing the bus to come, but when the bus did pull up at the stop, she suddenly remembered the workmen in the barn.

She would be going home to mess and tramping boots when all she wanted was the time to think things through. The bus doors hissed open and a cloud of warmer air enveloped her.

'Are you getting on?' asked the driver, as she hesitated.

'No. Sorry,' said Rowan. She walked away across the square and then, on an impulse, took the steep path down to the river.

It was even colder on the bank side. The wind blasted across the river towards her, picking up the damp chill of the water on the way. Rowan hurried along the muddy path until she reached the weir. She stopped there, watching the water flow over the lip of the weir with a smooth, muscular power. When it surged over hidden rocks, it twisted into thick ropes which looked solid enough to be picked up and hauled in dripping lengths to the bank. The river was high and the water was so full of churned-up mud, it looked like milky coffee. The sparkling shallows they had played in through the live-for-ever summer had been swallowed by the brown flood.

Rowan slid a sideways glance upstream at the rusty sewage pipe. She heard Sally's high voice call faintly.

'Walk across and you'll live for ever!'

Quickly, Rowan looked away. She thrust her hands in her pockets and continued her walk until she reached the gentle mound in the bank that marked the underground path of the pipe.

The high voice called in her head again, but this time, the promise had changed.

'Walk across and you'll win the case!'

Rowan stopped. The wind stopped too, and the first flakes of snow began to drift down from the grey sky. Rowan turned and gazed along the length of pipe to the opposite bank. The back of the pipe curved treacherously and the flakes of snow were coming down faster now, melting on the metal and giving it a greasy sheen.

'Walk across and you'll win.'

'Walk away and you'll lose.'

No. Rowan shook her head. That was a ridiculous idea. She tried to walk on but the superstition held her now, as strongly as the cracks in the pavement and the ghost curtains had gripped her when she was ten.

Rowan turned and stepped out onto the pipe. She felt the vibrations from the weir rumbling through the metal. 'Walk across and win,' she said, fixing her eyes on the far bank. 'Walk across and win. Walk across and win,' she chanted, stretching her arms out for balance. She began to walk, heel to toe, heel to toe, chanting all the way. She cleared the first joint, and then the second, carried forward by the rhythm of the chanting, but the vibrations running through the pipe were getting stronger.

Rowan felt her feet begin to slow. The pipe was really shaking now, as she reached the middle of the river. She stared fiercely at the bank ahead of her and willed her feet to keep moving on, but they came to a stop.

Rowan looked down at her feet and saw the brown water, rushing past below the pipe. It seemed to her that the pipe was moving, not the water. The pipe was racing upstream, rolling and shaking, and she was going to fall! Quickly, she shut her eyes but that made the whirling dizziness even worse. She could feel herself tipping off the pipe, her balance gone.

Rowan screamed and staggered, windmilling her arms. Then she dropped onto her belly and clung to the freezing metal, digging her fingers in and gripping with her knees until the giddiness stopped. She felt sick. Her bones ached with cold.

At last, she raised her head and fixed her eyes, once

again, on the opposite bank. Don't look down this time, she told herself. She eased from her knees to her feet and slowly straightened up until she was standing. She took one step, then another. The rhythm came back and on she walked, heel to toe. The far bank drew nearer until, at last, there was earth beneath the pipe instead of water.

'Yes!'

Rowan turned on the grass at the end of the pipe and stared across the river. She had done it! The pipe stretched out in front of her, as broad and flat as a pavement. Looking at it now, she could see that it really was wide enough to run along. Without thinking, she rose up on her toes and sprang forward. Her boots clanged onto the pipe and she raced across, yelling at the top of her voice all the way back to the other side. She rolled down the grassy bank, whooping with laughter, jumped up again, punched the air, then came to a sudden stop.

In that moment of clear-headed exhilaration, she realized there was a way to win. There was a way to take back their lives, even if they lost the case. Rowan's eyes widened as the answer slotted into place in her head like a line on a fruit machine.

Ching! She saw Eleanor standing in the witness box in her unsuitable suit and scraped-back hair.

Ching! She heard Eleanor's puzzled voice echoing round the court room, saying 'No. Not angry.'

Ching! She saw the wall of glass in the barn, its clean lines shrouded in blankets.

Rowan smiled, suddenly understanding what needed to be done. Eleanor had to stop living by other people's rules. She had to find her anger.

Rowan put her head down and began to run through the thickening snow. When she reached the square, she did not wait for a bus but kept on jogging steadily up the hill towards the barn. The answer

165

glowed in her head like an ember in a box and she knew she had to get home before it cooled.

She nearly lost it. The struggle up the hill through the blizzard took so much energy that she nearly let the cold misery of the barn reduce her answer to ashes. Then she looked at the new brick wall which the workmen had begun to build against the terrace windows. The wall was so wrong, so against the life they used to have, it set her answer glowing again. The wall had to come down.

She picked up the sledgehammer and swung it, ignoring Eleanor's shouts of protest. It hit the bricks with a dull thud and the shock of the contact spread through her arms and shoulders in a punishing wave. But the bricks had moved! The wet mortar could not hold the shape. Rowan grunted, heaved up the sledgehammer and swung it in a low arc to thud into the wall again. The bricks bellied outwards, further with each swing, until a whole section of wall fell into the drifting snow on the terrace. The wind howled through the hole and snow swirled into the room. Rowan laughed aloud, her eyes shining.

Eleanor darted in and grabbed her by the arm. 'Stop! Stop! What are you doing?' she cried, flinching as another brick fell.

'Have you got to go again, tomorrow, to the court?' panted Rowan.

'What's that got to do with it?'

'Have you?'

'Yes,' said Eleanor and Rowan grinned. It was not too late, then.

'I was there today, Mum.'

Eleanor's face crumpled and she sat down in the plaster dust in her smart suit and cried.

'Oh, no. I didn't want you to see that. I didn't want my daughter to see that.'

'No, but listen Mum, I'm glad I saw it because it made me realize something. You're right. Jeff Mason is going to get off. That shark Carver is going to make sure of it. You could stand on your head in the witness box and it wouldn't make any difference.'

Rowan stopped for a moment and looked down at Eleanor. 'But we don't have to lose everything, Mum. We don't have to wall ourselves in. We don't have to live by their rules. Their rules are going to let a guilty man go free, so why should we let them tell us how to live our lives?'

Eleanor had stopped crying. She sat absolutely still, listening.

'We can take our lives back, Mum,' said Rowan, softly. 'If we do that, we'll beat them. Because they won't get what they want, then, will they? Jeff Mason and Mr Carver and the women in the gallery and the kids with the paint and the voice on the phone – they want to see us hiding away, as though we were the guilty ones. Why should we let them get what they want?'

Eleanor looked up at Rowan and Rowan held her gaze. She felt as though she was slowly reeling Eleanor in from the bottom of a deep, dark well. The line was very thin. It could so easily snap.

'Mum? It's time to take your life back. Tomorrow, you go into the court in your own clothes, right? Wearing your perfume. And don't let Carver touch you! Don't let him make you ashamed of your life. Our life. You've got to get angry, Mum. You haven't been angry enough, all these months. You should be furious with the whole lot of them.'

Rowan held out the sledgehammer. She held it out for so long that her arms began to shake. Slowly,

slowly, Eleanor stood up, her eyes never leaving Rowan's. She took the sledgehammer.

'You're right,' she whispered.

Rowan nodded and stepped back.

Eleanor looked down at the sledgehammer, then hefted it onto her shoulder and faced the wall. With a savage yell, she brought the hammer down on the bricks and sent another section of wall tumbling out onto the terrace.

'Yes! You're right,' she shouted, throwing her arms around Rowan and hugging her fiercely as the snow and brick dust whirled around them.

'We win!' cried Rowan, exultantly.

SEX CASE LECTURER APPEARED IN NUDE STAGE SHOW

SEX CASE TUTOR 'A SLUT' SAYS LAWYER

LECTURER LEFT HOME-ALONE DAUGHTER FOR WEEKEND AWAY

SEX ASSAULT CLAIM AN ATTEMPT TO BLACKEN BOSS'S NAME

168

'Perhaps we should hide these?' said Margaret, hearing Eleanor clatter down the stairs. She began to gather the papers from the kitchen table, but Rowan stopped her.

'No,' said Rowan. 'She needs to see them. She's practising being angry.'

Eleanor came into the room wearing a dress of blue wool which flowed around her like water, and a green cashmere scarf. Her hair was loose and seemed to crackle with the energy she was giving off. Margaret and David gaped. Rowan breathed in the scent of her perfume and smiled.

'Nice,' she said.

Eleanor hardly glanced at the headlines. 'Let's go,' she said, grabbing her car keys.

'But – we don't need to be there until ten,' said Margaret.

'I have to go to the college first,' said Eleanor, opening the door.

'Why?'

'To tell them what they can do with their job!' yelled Eleanor, striding through the snow to the car. 'Old camel face is going to have to get his suit dry-cleaned after I've finished with him!'

A delighted smile slowly spread across Margaret's face. 'I don't know what you did, Rowan,' she said, 'but it worked. It worked!'

'Will somebody please tell me what is going on?' asked David.

'She's back,' crowed Margaret.

'And she's angry,' added Rowan. 'Come on, we're all going to court together today. Front row seats. This is going to be an amazing performance.'

They drove up to the moor, the day the verdict came out. Eleanor parked the car and they walked to their favourite rock outcrop, overlooking the valley. It was a beautiful winter day; still and clear, with a high, blue sky. They sat in silence for a while, looking across the valley at the tiny figures of the reporters as they scurried around the barn, hunting for a quote.

'The local rag is going to have a field day,' said Rowan. 'They've supported him all along.'

'Well, what do you expect? You know where the editor lives—'

'Bickersford Hill,' they chanted in unison.

'Nothing will ever be the same,' said Eleanor suddenly, and her voice was full of anguish. Rowan reached out and gripped her hand. Eleanor looked down and rubbed her thumb back and forth across the knuckles. Her tears fell warmly onto Rowan's skin.

'I need to ask you something, sweetheart,' said Eleanor. 'Will you give me an honest answer?'

'I'll try.'

'OK. I'm going to be all right, you know. I've got my new job in the city. I don't need to have anything to do with Bickersford if I don't want to. But you, you've got to go to school. You'll be there every day. What I want to know is, do we go or do we stay? It's your choice.'

Rowan thought hard. Eleanor was right, nothing would ever be the same. Eleanor had changed. She had been magnificent in court, that final day. She had been brave and angry ever since. But there was a new wariness about her which Rowan suspected would never disappear.

And their life here would never be the same. How could it be? But at least they knew how things really were. They knew their friends and their enemies now – most people could only guess at such a thing.

Then there was the barn, perched on the valley side with the restored glass wall glittering in the sun.

Rowan looked down at it and could not imagine living anywhere else. She thought about Sally, still at school, still struggling through. She thought about David and the way he looked at her with his gold-flecked eyes. How could she leave all that?

'We stay,' she said.

Eleanor took a deep breath. 'In that case,' she said, 'we'd better get back to the barn.'

'What's the rush?' asked Rowan, taking her mother's outstretched hand.

'We have a cake to bake,' smiled Eleanor.